# Barbie & Benz 3

# A Thug Love Story

## By

# Princess Diamond

**Twitter & Instagram**: @authorprincess
**Facebook**: @authorprincessdiamond
**Pinterest**: princess diamond

# Acknowledgements

I give all praises to God who anointed me with this wonderful gift of writing. Through Christ I can do all things.

To my father in heaven, you passed away too soon. You have never seen any of my work, but I write in your loving memory. Love you forever.

To my mother in heaven, I still can't believe you're gone so soon. I miss you every day. I wish you were here with me. My biggest supporter. Love you always. .

To my family and friends, I couldn't have done this without your endless days of listening to me talk about my stories, offering great ideas, and giving me awesome advice. You all are my rock. Thanks for everything.

To all the authors that have helped me. Much love and continued success.

To my readers, without your support, there is no me. I appreciate you all.

A special thanks to my sister. You are my number one fan. Your opinion is priceless.


XOXOX
Princess Diamond

# ♕ Princess Diamond's Books ♕

*Element of Surprise*

*Element of Surprise 2: Lust Unleashed*

*Put My Name On It*

*Dream & Drake Series 1-4*

*Everybody's Got A Secret Series 1-4*

*A King Pin Stole My Heart Series 1-3*

*Fallin For A New York Boss*

*Issa Hood Love Story: Tokyo & Greek*

*Hoodwives & Rich Thugs 1 & 2*

*This Thug Love Got Me Trippin: A Belize Christmas*

*Hooked On That Thug Love 1 & 2*

*Lovin A ChiTown Dope Boy 1 & 2*

*Desiree & Diablo 1-3*

*Thug Love: The Ultimate Box Set Collection*

*An Autobiography Of A Hitta's Wife*

# Chapter 1

## Brysen "Benz" Sorensen

Any minute now, my vehicle was going to catch on fire. I was at a loss. What should I do next? Everything I needed to break the window was inside the car. My nerves were shot to hell already. I was ready to smoke ten cigarettes at one time when I heard Mally start to cry. My headache worsened when my nieces started to cry too. Meanwhile, Barbie remained knocked out inside the car.

I wanted to be a hero and save my girl, but I put my pride to the side and called 911. All this bullshit had me thinking about the baby on the way. What kind of father would I make? This was a prime example of how irresponsible I am. I was about to give up and choose my nieces and nephews over Barbie. She would be missed dearly. Silently, I said a quick prayer for my bestie before I was about to walk away.

"Yo!" I heard someone call out.

I wiped the lone tear that was about to fall and put my

game face on before I turned around. The teen that I saw not that long ago who let me use his phone when I was stranded at Dache's crib was approaching me. He had a gun on his waist and a crowbar in his hand.

"I see you got your car back. You need some help?"

"Hell yeah," I beamed. "I'm glad to see your young ass."

"I got you, yo. I saw the whole thing," he exclaimed. "I called 911 as well. The fire department should be here any minute no2."

"I don't think we can wait for them. The car is about to be on fire any minute now."

"Nah, we ain't waiting on their asses. I was just letting you know that I called them. Until they arrive, we're going to work on getting your girl out."

He shot the back window out and the bullet bounced off. It put a slight dent in the back window, but nothing more than that.

"The fuck," he exclaimed.

"Bulletproof windows," we both said at the same time.

I liked this kid. I just wished we met under better circumstances. It seems like I was always in trouble whenever we bumped into each other. I sighed, feeling helpless.

"I know that look. Don't give up. We're going to get her out. I promise."

"Shit is looking slim."

"True, but it's not over until the fat lady sings, and that

2

bitch is about to blow like KeKe Wyatt. I have an idea. If I can remove the wires from one side, do you think you can reach inside and grab your girl?"

"I can try. That's for damn sure."

"Cool. Give me a sec."

The light-skin pretty boy jogged back to his ride and came back with a broom. "This might work."

"What are you doing with a broom in your ride?"

He smirked. "Don't ask."

"I won't. I'm just glad you have it."

The teen used the broom to move one of the wires to the other side of the car. He stood in place holding the broom while I opened the driver's side door and climbed in to get Barbie. She was slumped over with a bloody knot on her head. I scooted into the car, leaning in as far as I could, trying to grab Barbie. Her body didn't move. That's when I realized that she had her seat belt on. I'm glad she did. She might have gone through the windshield if she didn't.

"Hurry up, bro. I can't hold this wire much longer," Kapri struggled.

"I'm trying," I stated frantically, trying to unlock the seat belt. "The shit is stuck."

By now, my nieces had left their brother off to the side as he cried hysterically. They were trying to get back in the car with me. Each one was holding on to one of my legs as they both cried. I guess they assumed I was about to leave them. They didn't know, but that's something I would never do. I would never abandon them no matter what. With Malice being out of it, I was their substitute father. I intended to uphold my obligation.

"The car just caught on fire. Get her out before we all blow the fuck up."

"I'M TRYING DAMMIT!"

"TRY HARDER OR YOU, ME, HER, AND THE KIDS WILL BE ASHES."

The fuckin' seat belt was jammed. No matter how much I pulled on the muthafucka it wouldn't budge. I remembered my knife in the glove compartment and quickly opened it, retrieving the sharp object. Flicking the switchblade open, I used it to cut the seat belt and free Barbie.

"IT'S ABOUT TO BLOW!" Kapri hollered

The teen dropped the broom and scurried away from the car. Meanwhile, I managed to get Barbie out of the car.

"I need you two to run. Can you do that for, uncle?" I asked my nieces while securing Barbie in my arms.

They both nodded, and I prayed like hell that they could keep up. The teen grabbed Mally, and all of us hauled ass down the street, hoping that we got away from the car before it blew up. My nieces surprised me, running just as fast as we were. Shit, they looked like two gold medalists, nearly passing us by. None of us stopped until we got to the end of the street. That's when I heard the sirens, and the fire truck pulled up moments later.

"Now, these bitches show up," the teen exclaimed, out of breath. "I called these bastards a while ago."

"I know right," I said, looking back at my car that was in flames. "This is where our tax dollars go."

"Bitches," one of my nieces said.

"Bastard," the other one exclaimed.

"No. No. Bad word.'

They both giggled, and I realized that they weren't affected by this situation at all. Even Mally had stopped crying. I guess they knew they were safe.

"You know, I never got your name."

"Kapri."

"Thanks, Kapri. I owe you one man."

"Nah. You don't owe me. I was glad I could help. You seem like a cool dude. It would have been a shame for you to lose your girl or these cute little ones. You're a good father."

"Nah, man. These ain't my kids. They're my brother's kids. However, he's at the hospital right now in a coma, so keeping his kids safe means a lot to me."

"No doubt. Family is important, you know. I ride for mines just like you."

"That's what's up."

A fireman walked over along with two paramedics. The

EMT's pulled up a few seconds ago.

"Is everyone okay?"

"No," I voiced. "A car ran the light and struck my car. I hit that pole, and my girl is pretty banged up."

"Let me take a look," the male EMT said.

He took Barbie out of my arms and placed her on the stretcher. The two men checked her vitals and then rushed her to the ambulance.

"Hey. Be careful. She's pregnant," I yelled.

"Congratulations, bro," the teen applauded.

"Don't congratulate me yet. I don't know if the baby is mine."

"Damn, your girl is out there like that?"

"Nah. That's not what I meant. We weren't together at the time. I did some stupid shit. Then she did some stupid shit."

"Yo, I can relate. I'm always doing some stupid shit. Pussy will make you lose your mind."

"You can say that again."

"Are you riding in the ambulance with her as we transport her to the hospital?" the paramedic asked.

"Um," I looked back at my niece and nephew.

"Don't worry about them. I'll trail you. My car is right over there."

I was still skeptical. I didn't know this nicca. He seemed cool and all, but shit, he could be a child molester and kidnap my nieces and nephew.

He must've sensed my hesitation. "I know you don't know me, but I mean well. Here, I'ma give you my phone. I'll get it back when you get to the hospital."

"Not good enough. It could be a burner."

"True. Damn. You got a point." Kapri patted himself down. "I can give you my ID. I don't have my license. My shit got confiscated. I got tickets; you feel me. That's why my car was towed that night. Twelve always fucking with me because I be having nice shit."

"Damn and you're still driving around? Your ass is a hazard."

"Nicca don't judge me. I'ma get it back tomorrow after I pay the damn fines."

"I think my nieces and nephew are going to ride in the ambulance with me. They'll be safer. No offense."

"No, the fuck you didn't. That's some cold ass shit, yo."

I couldn't help but laugh. He was a silly ass dude. I could tell that he was hilarious without even trying to be.

"Hit me later."

"Aight. Bet. What's your number?"

I rattled my shit off, and he typed it into his phone. "I ain't never get your name?"

"Benz."

"Cool. I'll be in touch, Benz."

## Princess Diamond

The paramedics were impatiently waiting as I ran over to the ambulance. I helped the girls in, and then I got in next with Mally. I stared at Kapri as the doors closed. His ass was always there when I needed him. I had a feeling it was for a reason. I wasn't sure what the reason was, but time would tell. So far, I got a good vibe from him.

# Chapter 2

## Barbie Bennett

I felt as if I was falling. The best way to describe the feeling had to be close to the way the guy felt in the movie *Get Out*. I felt as if I was trapped inside of my own body. I heard Benz's voice. I heard another guy's voice. I assumed he was a friend of Benz. Although I wasn't sure. Mally and the girls were crying. Everything was a mess.

Benz kept calling my name as if he couldn't reach me or something. I wondered if I was dead. Is that why Benz's voice sounded so far away each time he spoke. I called out to him and yet I couldn't reach him, or maybe he couldn't hear me. I was so uncertain about everything.

The still small voice that I heard kept saying fight. I was trying as hard as I could to stop falling. Every time I tried to speak, it felt as if I was gurgling on my own blood. Machines, a baby's cry, and a horn honking replayed in my mind. Where was I? I had no idea, and I was scared senseless. Was I stuck in an alternate reality? Or was I really dead?"

"Pulse rate is dropping," I heard a man say.

Was he talking about me? I had no idea. I could only assume he was trying to help me.

"Barbie," I heard Benz say. "You saved me when I was passed out in front of my place after the fire. Now, it is my turn to return the favor. You are pregnant with child. I need you to fight. Come back from whatever place you have gone to. You need to be here with us. The people who love you. Not just for the baby, but for me too. Please. Barbie."

"Her blood pressure is almost stable," the guy helping me said. "And her heart rate is normal."

He had to be a paramedic.

What Benz said definitely made a difference because I finally opened my eyes, gasping for air.

"Damn, B, you scared the shit out of me," Benz said, staring at me with a huge grin.

"Benz, it's so good to see your face right now."

We glared at each other happy that we were both okay. I thought I was out of the woods until I felt a sharp pain in my stomach. It hit me so hard that I screamed for dear life, scaring the kids.

"Barbie!" Benz screamed. "What's wrong?"

"I don't know," I cried.

The paramedic sprang into action. "Where does it hurt?"

"My stomach,' I cried. "It feels like something is ripping through me."

The kids started to cry. Benz gave the girls his phone to play with and Mally a piece of candy. He was quiet, smacking his lips on the sugary treat. All three of them forgot all about my anguish since they were occupied with something else.

"Is she going to be okay?" Benz asked with worry.

"We're not sure," the paramedic replied. "The good part is we're at the hospital now so we can find out what's going on.

I was curled up in pain when the ambulance doors opened. The paramedic filled the hospital staff in on my issue.

"First-trimester pregnancy. She was unconscious on the scene. We're having trouble keeping her stats up."

Benz helped the girls out of the ambulance and snatched Mally up. All four of them ran side by side with the stretcher that wheeled me into the emergency room. The girls thought it was some sort of game, racing to keep up with the stretcher as I was being rolled into a room. Benz looked winded as he carried Mally's big butt, trying to keep up.

I wanted to laugh, but I couldn't. I was in way too much pain. Benz was going off.

"I ought to beat Malice and Behati's ass," he complained to no one in particular. "Your butt should be walking by now, Mally. If your parents didn't spoil you, you wouldn't be handicapped in a car seat. Your heavy behind would be running with your sisters."

The hospital staff ignored Benz as he fussed at his non-walking nephew. Once I was wheeled into the room, my shirt was lifted. Gel was put on my stomach and a wand was used to view the baby. The doctor moved it around a long time while staring at the screen.

"What's going on?" I stammered.

The doctor started moving the wand around again. I was wondering if he heard anything because I didn't.

"Is the baby okay?" I asked frantically.

No one answered my question, acting as if I hadn't said a word.

My stomach began to cramp. I screamed out in pain. "Aaahhhhh."

The pain knocked the wind out of me. This shit was far worse than any period or cramps. It felt as if the baby was going to fall out of my coochie.

"Give me some drugs," I pleaded. My request fell on deaf ears as the medical staff continued to look at the machines and then back at me. "Please," I begged. "The pain is too much. It hurts so bad."

"She's losing a lot of blood," one of the doctors announced.

Another doctor just joined along with another nurse.

"She's hemorrhaging," the doctor tending to me said. "Prep the OR, and I need blood on standby too."

The pain increased. I was delirious as the pain went up a notch and my breathing became labored. One of the nurses put an oxygen mask over my nose.

"What's happening?" Benz questioned frantically. "Why is she being prepped for surgery."

I groaned. "Benz," I called out.

He rushed to my side, holding my hand. "I'm here. Right by your side."

"I squeezed his hand. "I'm scared, Benz."

"I know. Silently pray like you told me when my mother was sick. Be strong and lean on God, okay?"

I nodded and took my own advice. I was glad Benz was there because I was scared.

"The baby is outside of her uterus. We need to stop the bleeding," the doctor said.

I hugged Barbie as she cried profusely.

"Be strong. You got this. I'll be here waiting for you after the surgery."

I used all of my strength to hug Benz. I didn't want to let him go, but I had to. Two nurses pried me from his embrace, putting the oxygen mask back on my face. Tears streamed from my face to my neck as they rushed me into surgery.

I was nervous. I'd never been pregnant before. As soon as I came to terms that I might be expecting, I was about to lose the life that I was carrying. They didn't say that I was losing the baby, but in my heart of hearts, I knew that I was. The cramping, the pain, and the complications indicated that my bundle of joy wasn't going to make it.

Maybe it was for the best. I didn't know who the father was. Archie claimed that it was his. Benz wasn't for sure about the conception. Deep down inside, I felt as though this was Benz's baby. Regardless, of the father, it was my baby. I wouldn't have risked his or her life no matter what obstacles I might have had to face. Until now, I didn't know if I wanted to be a mother. I guess now that I was facing a hard reality of losing my baby, I realized how much I wanted him or her to live.

# Chapter 3

## Archie Abney

Benz whipped my ass like I stole something. I never saw that ass whipping coming. My face was bloody and bruised. I just hoped that he hadn't broken my nose or jaw because my face hurt like hell. My phone rang and I side-eyed it. This wasn't the right time.

"Are you good? You haven't checked in for a while."

I sighed. "Yes, I'm good, but if you keep on calling me, I'ma end up in a damn box. What do you want anyway?"

"Don't boss up on me, mister. Meet me downstairs."

"Downstairs, where?"

"I'm at the hospital. I followed you here when you didn't return my phone calls. I'm right outside the emergency room exit smoking a cigarette."

I didn't need this shit right here. I planned on getting a few bags of ice, dumping them in my cousin's bathtub, and soaking for hours before going to bed. As usual, shit just wasn't going as planned. I walked out of the emergency room doors and saw this bitch standing there smoking just like she said.

"I'm here now what?"

"Meet me in the parking garage. Ten minutes. Second level. You know what my car looks like."

Detective Rashan walked away. I wanted to strike a match and set her ass on fire. She was the ultimate pain in the ass. If it wasn't for her, I wouldn't be in this predicament. She had me out here foul. All I wanted to do was stay low key and live my boring life.

"What do you have for me?" Detective Rashan asked as soon as I got into her car.

"Nothing. Like I told you before, Benz is smooth. It's going to take a lot more than just hanging around Barbie to get information on him."

"I don't think you're trying hard enough. I want to take this bastard Benz down."

"I know you do, but if you don't chill, my cover will be blown. Benz isn't as stupid as you think."

"He's stupid enough.," she added.

"How?" I questioned. "That man has outsmarted you and everyone else that you've put undercover to bust his ass. He's not a dummy like you think."

"That's why I have your ass Archie, or should I call you by your birth name Eddie?"

"Listen, I'm grateful for what you did for me, but if you want this plan to work, you need to fall back and let me handle this."

"Why? Tell me why I should do that?"

"Because Barbie thinks she's pregnant by me."

"You slept with her?"

"No, dumbass. That was my only leverage to stay around. Before I got my ass kicked by Benz, I found out that Barbie was pregnant. Of course, it's his baby, but I lied about the night we spent together, insinuating that the baby was mine."

Detective Rashan clapped her hands. "Oh, that's a good move. You're quick on your feet."

"I know. That's why you need to trust me."

"I don't know if I'll ever trust you. At any point, I know if you can save your own ass, you'll throw me and the rest of the department under the bus."

I laughed. She had a point. I might be snitching to them, but at the end of the day, I wasn't going to risk my life with Benz to save their asses. They wanted him, not me. I was just doing what I had to do to save my own ass.

"Listen, you little punk. I can send you right back where you came from if you don't cooperate with me like you agreed."

"I highly doubt it."

"So now you're a smart ass? I guess this is the thanks I get for saving your ass from the hood."

"Are we done?" I asked her. I was tired and in pain. I had no interest in talking to her any longer.

"We're not done, but you can leave. I'll be in touch."

"Whatever," I said, getting out of her rusty car. "I hope this isn't your real car. It had better be a work vehicle."

"Don't worry about my car," she urged. "You just make sure you keep your face away from Benz's fists."

With a hearty laugh, she pulled off. I knew I was in too deep with this mess. I wasn't a snitch, nor was I the fake ass nerdy dude that I pretended to be. The truth was my real name was Eddie Green. I grew up in a rough neighborhood on the Southside in poverty and crime like most poor, young black men.

I was into all types of shit. Grand theft auto, robbery, drugs, and anything else that paid the bills. Both my parents were addicts. They smoked up everything we had, so I did what I had to do to survive and take care of my siblings. All I had in this world was my little brother Lud and my baby sister Netta. My parents were crackheads. They never cared about us. Drugs were their only children.

I hadn't seen them since I got busted. That's how all this shit started. Detective Emily Sue Rashan busted my crew and me with a shit load of drugs, money, and guns. I was looking at life in prison when she presented me with the deal of a lifetime. She said no jail time, but I had to be her informant on the streets, which meant I had to snitch on all the street niccas she wanted to lock up.

I was cool with my deal at first. I got a name change. I went from Eddie Green to Archie Abney. I had a fresh start, and I took full advantage of it. I got my certification in real estate and turned my life around. Within no time, I was a new dude with a career, money in the bank, a fresh ride, and a sweet place to stay. Nobody knew the old me. I was free to do as I pleased.

However, there was a catch or two. I had to lose all contact with my old life, which included my mother, father, brother, and sister. As if that wasn't hard enough starting over as a new person alone, I was a bitch for Chicago PD. Basically, I went undercover so to speak, and spoon-fed information to the police department about criminals that were hard to catch. Benz was my latest conquest. He'd been on their radar for years, but they could never get enough information on him. Since I worked with Barbie, I was a sure bet to help them put him away once and for all.

The whole idea seemed simple. I wish it was. A few things stood in the way. I was in love with Barbie. I always have been, since the moment I saw her. Then there was the fact that Benz was careful. He didn't make many mistakes. I could get him on threatening me or some low-level bullshit but getting information on his drug empire was nearly impossible. The nicca was good.

At this point, I just wanted to marry Barbie, get her pregnant for real, and whisk her far away from Chicago so we could live happily ever after. We could start over in a new city as husband and wife with our kids and open our own real estate business together.

I walked to where my car was parked and hit the button to unlock the doors. Nothing happened. I turned my head left and right, realizing that the place where my car had been parked was now empty.

"I know I left my car right here," I exclaimed, pulling out my phone.

I was about to call Detective Rashan back and ask her to give me a ride after I called the police when someone hit me in the back of my head. I fell to the ground, knocked out cold in the same parking space where my car once was.

# Chapter 4

## Brysen "Benz" Sorensen

I was pacing in the hospital waiting room once again. Like déjà vu, I was wearing a hole in the hospital floors. A few hours ago, I was just here in a similar area scuffing up my shoes while I waited to find out about Malice's condition.

Now, once more, I was hoping and praying that Barbie and the baby were all good. No, I wasn't sure if the baby was mine. And yes, I hated Archie's bitch ass with a passion. Still, I could tell that Barbie wanted this baby. As much as I felt that it was a fifty-fifty chance that the baby was mine, I just couldn't stand in the way of something so beautiful being brought into this world. It was God's way of sprinkling earth with joy. No matter how much I hated Archie, I couldn't stand in the way of one of God's creations. Babies were blessings no matter how they were conceived.

Mama Bee and Chuck rushed into the hospital hysterically. After they were calmed down, they took a seat by Malice's kids.

We were all in the waiting room on pins and needles. Chuck was nodding off. Mama Bee had one eye on the kids with her pen in her hand, crossing out words in her puzzle book. A doctor walked into the waiting area, and I stopped pacing.

"I'm looking for the family of Barbie Bennett," he exclaimed.

"Right here," I confirmed.

He signaled me over. Chuck stood up and walked over to the doctor as well. Mama Bee stayed seated by the kids. Mally was sleep once again, and the girls were coloring in a gigantic book that one of the nurses gave them. They had a whole box of crayons to keep them occupied.

"Hi, I'm Dr. Swartz. We controlled the bleeding and got her stats under control. She's in ICU right now just as a precaution. We just want to keep an eye on her."

Chuck looked relieved, but I had a question.

"Um, what about the baby? Is the baby okay?"

Dr. Swartz looked from Chuck to me and held his head down. "I'm sorry. The baby didn't make it."

Chuck gasped, and I could tell that the news hurt him dearly. I had mixed feelings about the baby's termination. A part of me was glad that the baby didn't make it because I didn't know if it was mine or not. If the baby was Archie's, I knew that things would never be the same between Barbie and me ever again. He was a true fuck boy, and I was glad that Barbie was carrying no parts of his sorry ass.

However, on the other hand, the baby could have been mine. I was excited when I heard the nurse announce that Barbie was pregnant. Deep down inside, I felt the baby she was carrying was my seed. I wanted a boy. I was positive that Barbie and I would make great parents. We got along great, despite our new relationship issues. Being parents would have been the nudge that we needed to bring our love full circle.

"I'm not sure how Barbie will take the news when she wakes up," Dr. Swartz continued. "Of course, I can tell her if you'd like."

"No," I reassured. "I will tell her. She'll receive it better if it comes from me."

Dr. Swartz nodded passively. "I'll send someone when she opens her eyes."

"Thank you, doctor," Chuck acknowledged.

Dr. Swartz left, and I took a seat. Chuck was sitting in between Mama Bee and me.

"Are you alright?" Chuck asked me genuinely.

I let out a long breath. "Yeah. Today has just been one of those days. I keep replaying the car accident in my mind. I feel as if I could have done something more. Like, if I went another way or maybe I left the hospital a few seconds later."

"You said someone ran the light, correct?"

"Yeah. They did."

"Then, there wasn't anything more you could have done, son. You did your best. You have to be okay with that and let the rest go."

I heard him, but I was still beating myself up. I felt as if this was all my fault. "Barbie got hurt, tho. I will never be okay with that."

"She was hurt, but she's okay. You're okay. The kids are okay. From what you said, things could have gotten really ugly."

"What about the baby? Barbie just found out she was pregnant, and now she has to be told that she lost it."

"It's no one's fault. Sometimes things happen. If you want, I can tell her the news."

"No," I reassured him. "I can do it. Besides, I want to talk to her, comfort her, and see where her head is really at regarding the issue."

"Everything will work itself out, son. I promise."

"If you don't mind, can you keep the kids? If they keep Barbie, I'm going to spend the night with her."

"Of course. They can stay with us as long as you need them to."

"I appreciate that. With Malice being in a coma, his wife is here with him, and my dad is supporting them both; they don't have anyone else left to look after them except for me."

"We will gladly help you out. We're family. In a time of need, family sticks together. They will be just fine. You handle whatever business you need to and tend to Barbie. You can come and get them after things blow over."

"Thanks. I'm going to need the time to figure things out. I have a lot on my plate, and someone has to pay."

Chuck glared at me. "What is understood doesn't have to be explained. Handle your business, youngsta. Mama Bee and I have your back."

It was at that moment that I knew Chuck understood what I truly meant. He might have been an older fella, but he was from the streets. No, he didn't get down like I did, but he had several friends who did, so he knew what time it was. In so many words, he was giving me his approval to get to the bottom of this shit, by any means necessary. I intended to do just that. Muthafuckas were going to pay. Whoever thought they could hit me and get away with it was a dead man walking. Not only was the shit disrespectful, but it could have cost us our lives. Someone had to pay with their life for this shit.

Chuck sat next to me, looking off into space. I tinkered with my phone to keep my mind busy. Mama Bee kept up with the kids. She was a natural. I always wondered why they didn't have more kids. Life was crazy like that. It seemed like the people who loved kids didn't have any or only had one. The people who couldn't stand kids or didn't want any had a ton. That shit was unfair as hell.

Dr. Swartz popped back into the room. "She's up. You all

can see her. Only one at a time though."

Chuck and Mama Bee both looked at me. I hadn't intended on going first. Respectfully, her parents deserved to see her before me, but I followed Dr. Swartz to her ICU room since they insisted.

Barbie was sitting up with an oxygen tube in her nose. She looked out of it when I walked in.

"Hey," I whispered.

"Hey," she replied groggily. "What happened?"

"We were in a car accident. Some idiot ran the light and struck the vehicle on your side. You blacked out, regained consciousness, and then blacked out again."

Barbie leaned her head back on the pillow. "I remember some of it like I was watching a movie or something. It's all surreal. How's the baby?"

Aww man. I was hoping to ease into this conversation. I thought about lying now and telling her the truth later once she was well. Her curious eyes met mine, and I couldn't get my words together. The fib that I was about to let roll off my tongue wouldn't come out.

"The doctor said the baby didn't make it."

She looked disappointed.

"I know this is hard, but I'm just glad you made it."

"Are my parents here?"

I stared at her, doing a double take. She went from being

sad about the baby to the next subject as if she wasn't affected. Something wasn't right. She has to be in shock. There is no way Barbie would respond this way. It could be the drugs too. They did have to sedate her. Yeah, that's probably what it was.

I was about to walk out and get Barbie's parents when her eyes rolled into the back of her head. One of the machines she was hooked up lit up and started ringing loudly.

"Code Blue. Code Blue," the machine broadcasted loudly.

Dr. Swartz and a few other medical staff rushed into her room, moving me to the side. Barbie was knocked out again.

A nurse checked her vitals. "She just bottomed out."

Dr. Swartz pulled back the cover. The bed was covered in blood.

"She's hemorrhaging again. Call the OR and tell them to prep her again for surgery. Grab more fluids and bags of blood."

I was scared as fuck as Barbie crashed. They performed chest compressions on her until she had a heartbeat again. Then, they rushed her passed me out of the room, racing her into surgery.

I stood there for a moment, thinking about what I just saw. Barbie didn't deserve this. She was getting her ass kicked, and I felt guilty about it all. How could I tell her parents what just happened? More importantly, what if she didn't make it through the surgery due to all the bleeding. I can't imagine life without Barbie.

# Chapter 5

## Barbie Bennett

I woke up in ICU for the second time around. My body was achy, and I felt worn out due to the surgery. I had a minor incision near my navel that would remind me of this experience forever. However, I was told that my recovery would be almost instant. I was given an experimental drug that stopped the bleeding right away and my incision was held together by surgical glue. The doctor said that basically I would be in a little pain, but my body would be fully healed within twenty-four hours. I was sure that Benz had something to do with this. The special treatment that I received sounded very exclusive and expensive.

Benz was slumped over in the chair next to the bed with his arms folded across his chest. He had his jacket covering him like a blanket while he rested his head on his arm. I could tell that he'd been sitting there for quite a while. The way he was sleeping looking quite uncomfortable to say the least.

The doctor walked in, noticing that I was up. "Glad you're

awake, Miss Bennett. You gave us quite a scare."

I smiled weakly. "Am I okay?"

"Yes. You're doing fine." His eyes darted towards Benz. "Thanks to your boyfriend over there you will have s speedy recovery and you'll be as good as new."

"What happened? Why did I need to have a second surgery?"

"Unfortunately, you still had some placenta left behind. In these types of cases, it's hard to remove everything the first time around. Often times, in emergency situations like yours, we have to do a second surgery."

"That means I lost the baby, huh?"

The doctor nodded. "I'm sorry. The baby never had a chance. We had to focus on you. I hope you understand. You're a vibrant, young woman with your whole life ahead of you. From what I saw, nothing is stopping you from conceiving again. This was just a minor bump in the road towards your journey of motherhood."

The doctor patted my hand lovingly and then left.

"I know you're devastated," Benz said, stretching. He stood up and approached my bed.

"I'm fine," I replied sadly. "It's more mental than physical."

I wasn't fine, but I didn't want to put my sorrows on him.

"Besides, there was a possibility that it wasn't even your

baby, so thanks for staying. You could have left."

"Don't even start that pity bullshit. You know I wasn't leaving. I don't care if it was Archie's buck-tooth ass baby. I was going to be right by your side."

I started laughing, and pain shot through my side. I grabbed a pillow to brace myself from the shock of laughing. "You know you ain't right. Archie is not buck-tooth."

Benz cut his eyes. "I can't tell. That's how he looks to me."

"Has he come by? Does he even know that I'm here?"

"Shit. I don't know, Barbie. You act like I have that nicca's number or something. Why don't you call him?"

"Do you mind?"

"Nah. Call his punk ass, but if he gets out of line, I'ma put his ass in the room next to yours. He'll be needing medical attention just like you do."

I tried not to laugh again because I knew Benz was serious about hurting Archie. He hated him, and I was starting to see why when a bitch answered his phone.

"Who dis?"

I had to look at the phone to make sure I dialed the right number.

"I said, who dis?" the hoe asked.

"Is Archie available?"

"Girl, don't call here no more."

**CLICK!**

"Damn," Benz said. "You sure know how to pick 'em. That nicca ain't shit. You talk about me being a dog. I think he deserves the dog of the year award. You're in here laid up after losing his baby, well possibly his baby and this nicca is out there fucking around with the next bitch. Humph. Humph. Humph."

I felt so overwhelmed. My life was falling apart, and I couldn't do anything about it. Benz was right. I was stupid. Archie played me. He probably never cared for me. It was all a game just to put a notch on his belt or piss Benz off. He did seem in competition with Benz a lot. The fact that I was even in this predicament was unbelievable. I dismissed Benz to be with Archie, and this nicca treated me like a two-dollar hoe. All of a sudden, the brave front that I tried to keep up came crashing down. I was bawling hysterically about to bust my stitches.

"Aw shit. Out of all the times I asked you to listen to me, now you do it?"

"No, you're right, Benz. I was stupid, and now I'm paying for it. I should have listened to you from the beginning. Archie was never in my league."

"Shhhhh," Benz urged, sitting on the bed next to me.

"If you weren't here with me, I wouldn't have nobody."

"Your parents are a phone call away. They just left not too long ago with Malice's kids. If they weren't keeping them, they would have stayed. Besides, you were only allowed one visitor, and I am glad it is me."

"I feel so dumb," I cried. "I never wanted to be with Archie. I just wanted someone who wanted me. You didn't seem like you wanted me, Benz."

"I've always wanted you, Barbie. I just didn't think I was the best man for you. I never wanted you to go through this street bullshit with me. I got issues, as you know. I can't keep my dick in my pants, and I'm hot-headed with a quick trigger finger."

"I know that already, but if this baby were yours, you'd be right by my side like always. The man I picked abandoned his child and me. He didn't care if I lived or died. He played me for some pussy."

Benz wrapped his arms around me, and I fell into his chest, sobbing uncontrollably. I held him tight for dear life. His embrace felt like the only thing keeping me sane right now. I was so hysterical that I could hardly breathe.

"Barbie listen to me, take deep breaths before you have to stay in here longer than necessary."

Benz snuggled his body next to mine as I hyperventilated while taking his advice and trying to inhale and exhale as well. He held me in his strong arms as my breathing returned to normal. Mentally, I was still a mess, but at least I didn't feel as though I was having a panic attack.

"You can leave if you want to," I exclaimed, feeling as if I was holding Benz up from being somewhere.

32

"I know I can. You're not giving me permission to do shit. I'm here because I want to be. I'm not going to keep telling your ass that. Now, lay down and get some rest so you can get discharged when you're supposed to. All this crying and emotional shit will have your vitals going berserk. They gone keep your ass if you keep crying and feeling miserable. This about to be your permanent residence."

I leaned back in the bed, resting my head on the pillow once again. Benz kicked off his shoes and climbed in the bed with me. We barely fit in the bed together, but it was cool because I wanted him to be this close. I felt safe.

"I can order a movie if you like. We can make it a movie night right here."

"Can you order pizza too?" I asked. My eyes lit up because I was now hungrier than ever.

"I'll check with the doctor. If he says you can have pizza, then that's what I'll order."

"Thank you, Benz. You're the best."

Benz grinned. It wasn't his usual grin, but one that expressed relief and gratitude.

"No, you're the best, Barbie."

He kissed my cheek, sat up, put on his shoes, and went to ask the doctor what I could eat.

**\*•.‚♡ Barbie & Benz ♡‚.•\***

Opening my eyes, I expected to see Benz lying next to me. It was a wonderful surprise when I saw my mother sitting next to me instead. She was my shero growing up. My parents taught me everything that I knew. I was grateful to have wonderful loving parents like them.

"Where is Benz?"

"I told him to go home. He just left about fifteen minutes ago. I had to force that man to leave. I don't care what has happened between you two. I know that man loves you. Only a man who cares for a woman will stick around when he doesn't even know if the baby is his."

"Oh, ma," I cried.

"I picked the wrong man and look at me now. How do I come back from this? Benz isn't going to want me after this."

"That man wants you, and he always will. Do you see how he looks at you? He's crazy about you, Barbie. Why do you think he's always around?"

"Because we're best friends."

My mother got up and sat on the edge of my bed. Honey, you have a lot to learn about men. Yes, it might be true, he does value your friendship, but things are deeper between you two than what you think. Stop looking at it logically and go with your heart."

"But he hurt me, mama. I gave myself to him, and he

tossed my feelings in the trash."

"That might be how it looked at the time, baby. But I assure you, he was just as scared as you were."

I rested my head on my mother's shoulder. "How do you know, mama? Because that's not what I saw."

My mother let out a hearty laugh. "Don't ever tell him that I told you, but he came to me, honey. We talked. It was a long, drawn-out, deep talk. That man spilled his guts out to me about everything after the kidnapping. Tears and all."

"Tears?" I asked, raising my head from her shoulder. "But Benz doesn't cry."

"Honey, he was crying his eyes out like a one-year-old child. In fact, he sounded the same way you did a few minutes ago. Talking about, he ruined things between you two. He didn't mean to react the way he did after things crossed the line, and he was afraid of losing you. Benz is scared, that's all. Just as scared as you are. Now, it might be for different reasons, but you both share the same feelings. That bond."

My mother paused for a moment and smiled, shaking her head. "Oh my God, that bond. It's the work of the Lord. He brought you two together for a reason. I don't know what that reason is, and I don't understand the journey. What I do know is love. You two love each other unconditionally. That's all that matters. Stop holding him accountable for what has happened and let it go, baby. It's eating you alive. Give that burden to the

Lord, like I taught you."

"What about the baby?" I asked, getting sentimental all over again. I was in tears before I knew it.

"Let me share something with you. I'm not sure if this will make you feel better or not, but this is what God has put on my heart to say. You know how much your father and I love children."

"Yeah."

"You have asked me a million times for a brother or sister, and why are you the only child when we love kids so much. I never could bring myself to tell you the truth. I feel like now is the perfect time to share this with you. Your father and I met and married in less than six months. We were so in love, and we wanted to start our family right away. Well, the good Lord did not see things that way. We tried and tried and tried. Nothing happened for years."

"Oh, mama," I said, hugging her as tears gathered in her eyes.

"Don't be doing all that. I ain't never going to get the story out."

I handed her a tissue, and we both giggled because we were two crybabies.

"Finally, I got pregnant. We were so excited. We told everyone. Your father and I made a million plans for our new bundle of joy. And then, the unthinkable happened. We lost the baby. Just like you, I was in the hospital having a similar procedure, and your father was worried just like Benz was sitting in a chair like that. My parents and his parents were in the waiting room like we were waiting for you. Your father and I were so angry. We didn't know what we did to deserve such a loss. We were good people. Why did God forsake us?"

I hugged my mother, comforting her, wiping the tears that fell down her cheeks with tissue.

"But your father and I decided to love our way out of the situation. We focused on each other and building the lives that we wanted despite not having the children that we desired. And sure enough, one day, I got pregnant with you. Your pregnancy was perfect, but after having you, I almost hemorrhaged to death, and I had to have a hysterectomy. That's why you don't have any brothers or sisters. Baby, I tried so hard to have a house full of kids. It just wasn't possible."

My mother and I were holding on to each other, crying our eyes out. She was in pain, and I was in pain, but at least we had each other.

I kissed my mother on her teary cheek. "You and dad gave me a great life, and I wouldn't have it any other way. It would have been nice to have siblings, but maybe that would have interfered with my close relationship with you two. You're like my best friend, ma. I couldn't imagine having any other relationship with you."

My mother kissed my wet cheek. "I'm so glad you said that. I always felt guilty for not having someone for you to play with."

"Are you kidding? I have a million cousins. They were always around like sisters, especially Corset and Rozi. Then there is Xstaci. She and I are close even though she lives in New York Visiting her during the summer was priceless."

"That's true. I'm so glad we had this moment."

"Me too. I feel much better, and I know that God will bless me like he blessed you when the time is right."

"That's my baby girl speaking now."

"Oh lawd," my father exclaimed. "What have I walked into. You two are crying again. I need to invest in tissue just to save money because of you two."

My mother and I giggled. My father was always going in on us about crying so much. That was just his way of saying that he cared without sounding sappy too. My father walked over and sat my duffle bag in the seat. Then, he kissed me on the forehead.

"You're coming home with us for a while so we can nurse you back to health. I hope you don't have a problem with that."

"I don't, but what about Benz."

"He's right here," my father said, ushering Benz inside.

Benz walked into my hospital room, looking fresh. He was clean, and all dressed up.

"What's the occasion?" I asked, thinking that maybe someone had died or something. My eyes darted to his father and Behati standing in the doorway, and I feared that maybe Malice's health had taken a turn for the worse. My mother moved to the side, and Benz took her place, standing next to the bed. He grabbed my hand, and I braced myself for the bad news.

"Barbie, I'm sorry that you had to go through this. Once again, pain has occurred in your life, and you don't deserve it. When I saw all that blood, I thought I had lost you forever. I would have had a hole in my heart if you left this earth, and I didn't tell you how I really felt. I love you, and I never want to cause you pain ever again. However, I am human, and I'm learning, nonetheless. I hope you can accept me for who I am because I accept you, flaws and all."

He got down on one knee, and I realized what was happening.

"I wanted to do this a different way, but now is the right time. Everyone close to us is right here."

My eyes darted to the window in front of my room, and I saw Rozi, Sabre, and Corset.

"The baby that you lost," Benz continued. I want to go half on another one. This time I want you to conceive it as my wife. Barbie Bennett, will you marry me?"

"YES!" I screamed, feeling as if I busted my incision.

Benz put the ring on my finger as everyone cheered. He

stood, pecked me on the lips, and then hugged me.

"You know I'ma kill you right," I teased. "Did you really ask me to go half on a baby in front of my parents?"

Benz cracked up laughing, and I did too. I wasn't sad anymore. Thank you—God, for turning my pain into pleasure. I lost the baby but gained a fiancé. I was winning.

# Chapter 6

## Archie Abney

"Good Morning, Mr. Abney," the nurse said with a smile. "You're finally up."

"Where am I?" I asked, sitting up with a horrible headache.

"University of Chicago Hospital."

"What?" I questioned, making my head hurt even more. I held my forehead for a moment, trying to get my bearings.

"Don't stress yourself. Do you need something for pain?"

"Yes, please. My head is killing me."

Within moments, I was resting my eyes, sleeping for the next few hours. When I opened my eyes this time, Detective Rashan was sitting by my bedside.

"Well, it's about time. I thought maybe you were dead or something."

"That's not funny," I exclaimed. "I wouldn't be in here if you didn't pull off so fast. The shit happened right after you left."

"I'm not so sure."

"What is that supposed to mean?"

"Your car was in a hit and run."

"Well, it was stolen, so there's that."

"Are you sure it was stolen?"

"Listen, I'm not with the merry-go-round bullshit. Just say what you want to say."

"We have photos of you in the car, hitting Benz. After the hit and run, we found you and the car blocks away. You were passed out on the steering wheel. A neighbor called it in."

I couldn't believe this shit. "Wait. That's not what happened."

"Are you calling the camera light that snapped the picture, the paramedics that rescued you, and the neighbor that called for help liars?"

"Yes! I was laid out on the concrete with my head busted while you drove off into the sunset. What part of that don't you understand?"

"Let me show you since you don't believe me."

When she showed the pictures of what appeared to be me hitting Barbie and Benz after we all left the hospital, I was flabbergasted.

"I don't remember doing this," I said, staring at the pictures.

"Maybe the video will jar your memory then."

# Barbie & Benz 3

I watched as the detective pulled out her phone and played a video that was more shocking than the pictures. Apparently, I was driving at high speed and ran a light, striking the vehicle that Barbie and Benz were in.

"I still don't think that's me."

"The person has on the same clothes that you have over there," she said, pointing to the folded clothes in the chair.

"I don't care what you say. I will repeat it. That...wasn't...me."

"Unfortunately, Archie, that won't fly. You're going to have to come with me."

"Why? Am I even well enough to be released?"

"Right now, that's the least of your concerns."

"So, my health and safety isn't a concern? You sound crazy right now."

"No. What's crazy is I helped you get a deal, your identity changed, a new life, and you avoided jail time due to your criminal lifestyle. Yet, you haven't brought me any information on Benz."

"But I have brought you information on other niccas," I spewed.

"Calm down," Detective Rashan urged.

"Nah, fuck that. You calm down. I've been doing this shit for you for a hot minute. Snitching left and right. The one time I don't have information for you, you act as if I haven't provided you anything."

"Like I said, calm down. You work for me. I don't work for you."

"Work? Bitch, you don't pay me shit."

"Oh, there he is. Eddie Green coming to the surface."

"You damn right. I'ma always be Eddie Green."

"Put your clothes on Eddie, because we're about to take a little ride."

"What about my health?" I asked again.

"Depending on how things go, you might have twenty-four-hour healthcare."

The fuck did she mean by that? I was just about to ask her when her phone rang.

"This is important. I need to take this. You get dressed, and I'll be right back."

Headache and all, I jumped my ass out of bed and dressed in a snap. I knew this was my time to escape while Detective Rashan was occupied. While she was on the phone with her back turned, I slipped out of the room, swiftly walking in the opposite direction. I wanted to wait for the elevator, but I couldn't. As I hurried down the stairs, light-headed and all. A few times, I had to stop because I felt as if I was going to fall.

After catching my breath, I walked out of a side door. I didn't want to take any of the main entrances. I was afraid that Detective Rashan already had an A.P.B out on me. I still had my phone, so I hit up Jakoda. She was the only one that I could count on since Barbie and I were on the outs. Jakoda didn't pick up on the first ring, so I called her back immediately. I let that sucker ring until she answered.

"Hello!" she yelled.

"I need you to come and get me."

"Archie, are you crazy? Don't you ever in your natural-born life call me like that again unless it's an emergency."

"It's a damn emergency," I spat.

"If you're not dead, it's not an emergency. Besides, I'm busy. I had to fill in and take over your clientele because you didn't bring your black ass to work."

"It's an emergency. I was in the hospital. Can you come and get me?"

"I guess. Where are you at? What part of the hospital?"

"I left. I'm at Hyde Park Union Church."

"What are you doing there?"

"It's a long story. Are you on your way or what?"

"Don't get an attitude. I'll leave your sick ass where you are."

"Just hurry up."

"I'll get there as soon as I can."

Jakoda hung up on me, and I continued to walk towards the church. By the time I made it to the church, Jakoda was already parked waiting for me. I opened the car and got in.

"It took your ass long enough," she stated, pulling off. "Shit, I thought you were already here by the way you were spewing demands."

"I'm not in the mood for your shit, Koda."

"Are you in a good mood?" she asked sarcastically.

"I have every right to act the way I'm acting."

"Why? What happened to you?"

"Someone hit me in the back of my head, stole my car, ran a light, and hit someone."

"Damn. Are you okay?"

"No, I'm not. I might be facing jail time, and that's not even the half of it. You'll never guess who I supposedly hit."

Jakoda took her eyes off the road, staring at me briefly. "Who? Please don't say a cop."

"Worse. Barbie and Benz."

"Shut the hell up. You're lying," she exclaimed, getting louder.

"Nah. Unfortunately, I'm not."

"Damn. You fucked up. You know she was in the hospital too. She lost the baby and everything."

"What?" I nearly shouted. "She did?"

"Yep. I guess it's not so bad because Benz proposed afterward."

"Wow. That's fucked up."

"Not really. Now, you can focus on us."

"Koda, you know we don't have that type of relationship. As I told you, you want more from me than I can give you."

"Like what?"

"You have to ask?" I probed. "For one, you're very high maintenance. Secondly, you are jealous as hell. I don't want to wake up to both of my wrists being slit because you thought I cheated on you."

"Is that why you keep me as a booty call?"

"If you want me to be honest, yeah."

"Um, that's interesting. So, where am I taking you?"

"I was hoping that I could stay the night tonight. I can't go to my place until tomorrow."

I didn't want to tell her that I was dodging Detective Rashan because I was now on the run since, I was a person of interest.

"That's cool, but since you're not my man, you're going to have to run me my money."

"Say what? I've spent the night at your place before."

"True, but that was before you confessed that you won't see me as anything more than a piece of ass." She stuck out her hand. "I need five hundred."

"Wow. It's like that?"

"It's like that, bruh. Pay up, or I can drop your ass off at the next light."

I sighed. "You got it. I'll have your money tomorrow when

I go home. I don't have any money on me, and I lost my debit card in the midst of everything."

"That's cool as long as I get my money."

My plan was to spend the night with Jakoda and go home the next day when it got dark. I was going to pack, get my other ride and money. Pay Koda what I owe her and leave town. I had a nice little stash back at my crib. It wasn't enough to get out of the country, but it was enough for me to go into hiding. I refused to go back to jail.

# Chapter 7

## Brysen "Benz" Sorensen

"What color panties are you wearing? Show me."

I stuck my tongue out and licked my lips while watching Barbie on FaceTime.

She giggled. "You know your nieces are in here with me."

"Oh shit," I gasped. "I mean, shoot. I hope they can't hear me."

"Chill. They're sleeping. They've been knocked out for about twenty minutes or so. You're good. I was just warning you."

I sighed. "Whew! Malice would cuss my ass out if he heard me talking that way in front of his kids."

"Speaking of Malice. How is he doing?"

I frowned. "The same, but I have faith that he's going to pull through."

"Me too," Barbie agreed.

"Damn, you look good right now. Are you horny like I

am?"

Barbie giggled again. "Why do you want to know?"

"Because I want to slide deep in that. I can be there in ten minutes. Just let me in."

"I will not," Barbie laughed. "My parents will kick my butt."

"But we're engaged," I countered. "You're almost my wife."

"Almost doesn't count. And speaking of that—"

"Aw shit," I groaned. "Here comes the bullshit."

"What?" Barbie playfully asked.

"You know what. I can feel the other shoe drop as you speak."

"Well, now that you mentioned it. I was thinking—"

"Your thoughts better have something to do with you in a bikini, heels, and twerking."

"Hell no, it doesn't. You're out of your mind and nasty too."

We shared a laugh until Barbie paused. "Where are you?"

Before I could answer, she was grilling me once again.

"Please don't tell me you're at some bitch's house. Not after you proposed to me."

"No, Barbie, I'm not."

"I don't believe you. Let me see your surroundings."

I hesitated because I knew if I showed her where I was it

would be a problem. "You don't trust me?"

"Hell no," she exclaimed. "I love you, babe, but you're a hoe."

"A reformed hoe. Thank you very much."

"I'm not so sure."

"Why don't you believe me?"

"Because once a hoe, always a hoe."

"Damn. That's cold, Barbie. I thought you accepted my proposal because you trusted me."

"No. I accepted your proposal because I love you.'

"Ouch. That really hurt."

"As it should, now show me your surroundings. I know you're not at my place so where are you?"

Reluctantly, I took the iPhone off my face and showed her the bedroom that I was in. The new king-sized silver and black bedroom set with matching furniture shown on the camera.

"Where the fuck are you at?" Barbie questioned.

"Language in front of the kids," I urged.

"Where the F are you at? Answer my question before I show up over there."

Barbie was so cute when she was mad. I wanted to laugh in her face because she was overreacting, but I didn't want to get cussed out. Knowing her, she would probably take her ring off and end the engagement.

"I'm at home, boo. I swear to you."

"Prove it," she asked, sounding insecure.

I changed the camera of my phone to show her the room. From one end to the other, I showed her where I was.

"Let me see more," she exclaimed.

"You sound like a crazy person," I rebutted. "Don't get jealous on me."

"I'm not. I just need to see more. That doesn't look like your room."

"What do you expect? My shit was destroyed in the fire. I got all new furniture."

"Show me the rest of the place before I show up over there." Barbie barked. "I don't think you want that, do you?"

I exhaled. Barbie has been a basket case since she's been in the hospital. I'm starting to think that she hit her head harder than I thought she did.

"Fine. Whatever you say in the name of love."

"Don't pull no guilt trip shit on me. I meant what I said."

"Bruh, I'm doing this because I love you. Don't get it twisted." I exhaled again. "I'm nobody's punk, and I'm letting you control me this one time because I want to prove to you that you can trust me. But if you ever in your natural-born life ask me to do this again, I'm ride on you so hard you're going to regret everything that you ever knew."

Barbie twisted her lips in the camera. "Are you going to get on with it or nah?"

"I'ma get on with it, but just know that I'm doing this because of everything I took you through. This is to put your mind at ease and to never question me again."

I opened the door with Barbie watching on FaceTime.

"Why is it so dark?"

"Because I had all the lights out. I was in my bedroom. I didn't think that I would have to come out and prove some shit to my fiancée."

Barbie smirked. "Blah. Blah. Blah."

I was about to respond to Barbie's smart-ass remark when the light that I just cut on went out.

"Why is it dark again, Benz? Did you cut the lights out so I couldn't see that bitch at your house?"

I didn't want to alert her, so I calmly responded. "Baby, I'ma make me something to eat. Let me call you back?"

"So, you about to cook for some bitch?" Barbie snapped. "Where is she at? Let me see the hoe."

I didn't even entertain her bullshit. I hung up while she was in mid-sentence. I would deal with her antics later. Grabbing my .44, I crept downstairs with my gun as my eyes adjusted to the darkness. I had a suspicion that someone was in my crib. I'm assuming it was the same pussy ass nicca that set my shit on fire last time. I wasn't certain, but my gut was screaming that I was right on point. I followed my instincts as my .44 led the way.

Quietly, I crept downstairs towards the living room. That's

the direction that I assumed the burglar went towards. Slowly, I made my way to the bottom of the steps, taking a deep breath before I proceeded. It was dark as fuck, but I remembered my home like the back of my hand. It didn't matter that I hadn't laid my head here in weeks. Regardless of the fact, I knew my home. Someone was trespassing. I was prepared to fight or kill for what was mine.

There was movement. A dark shadowy figure. This shit felt like déjà vu. I wouldn't be surprised if this was the same person who broke into my house that night it was set on fire. Unlike last time, I was going to pop the dog shit out of this muthafucka.

I caught the bastard about to walk right out my front door. I guess the stupid ass person didn't realize that I was at home. It seemed like they were casing my place out or planting cameras or something.

**Click! Click!**

"Not tonight, bitch," I exclaimed. "You broke into the wrong muthafucka's house this time."

The intruder gasped. That's when I realized it was a woman. I felt like it was a woman last time, or a man dressed up like one. I let off a shot. I wasn't sure if I hit her or not, even though, she fell into the door, closing it with her body. In the darkness, I felt something whizz past my face. I could only assume it was a bullet. She must've had a silencer on her shit.

I wanted to cut the lights on, but I felt like I had a clear advantage in the dark. I knew my way around in the dark like a blind man. It was now or never. I had to take my shot. I didn't want to go completely off but fuck it. I let off three shots in her direction before going to the basement to cut the lights back on. Rushing back upstairs, I got the shock of my life when I saw who was laid out on my hardwood living room floor. I had to blink twice just to come to the realization of who I was seeing.

"Dache?"

She was sprawled out with a bloody spot on her stomach. Her mask rested on top of her head. In her left hand was a gun with a silencer. Her right rested over the bloody wound.

"I'm sorry, Benz," she exclaimed.

She coughed, and blood spewed from her mouth.

I ran over to her side, placing the fluffy rug that draped over my couch over her. "Why?"

She smiled, going into another coughing fit. "I wish we met under different terms, but we didn't. I was paid to break into your place and damage your computer."

"By who?" I wondered.

"Archie," she whispered before taking her last breath.

Her head fell over to the side, and that was all she wrote. I expected her to cough or fight or something. Nope. It was just like the movies. She inhaled a small breath and then released it before her body was lifeless.

I've taken many lives, but this one got to me. I didn't kill women or kids. Dache was a ratchet chick, but I didn't want her dead. The fact that she was contracted by Barbie's ex to kill me made me furious. It was time for Archie to go. I was about to call Traffik to come and clean up Dache's body when red and blue lights flashed through my living room.

"Dammit!"

I dimmed the lights and rushed to the window. Two fuckin' cops were coming up my walkway.

"Fuck!"

I had to think quick.

I drug Dache's bloody body into my hall closet. Quickly, I wiped up the little bit of blood that was on my hardwood floor. Just as I put my robe on, my doorbell rang. Casually, I put the chain on my front door and cracked it open.

"Hello. What's going on, officers?"

"We got two complaints. Someone said they saw someone in black walking around the neighborhood, and another person said they heard shots. We're were wondering if you saw or heard anything."

"Um, no officer, I haven't. I was sleep until the flashing lights woke me up." I faked a yawn and stretched for emphasis, hoping to make my point.

"Do you mind if we come inside and look around?" the other officer asked.

"Sure, if you have a warrant."

He grinned as if he had a trick up his sleeve. "Why would we need a warrant if you have nothing to hide."

"Why would you want to look inside of my place if I didn't see anything. I thought you were investigating a potential burglary. That was my assumption."

The officer stared me down as if he wanted to say something more, but he conceded. "Sorry about that. You're right."

"I know."

"Thank you for your time," the first officer stated as I closed the door in their faces.

What kind of fool did they think I was? They came knocking at my door asking if I saw something, and then they wanted to come inside and look around. That shit don't even sound right.

With the block being hot, I couldn't call Traffik to come over this way and risk getting hemmed up. I was going to have to dispose of Dache's body myself. It wouldn't be the first time I'd done clean-up work. However, I hadn't done this shit in a minute, so it took me a moment to get my routine together. I was rusty as fuck.

I placed her into a huge lawn tractor bag, I cleaned up the space where she was and waited for the officers to leave. I didn't want to get caught, so I waited another hour just in case. Then, I drug Dache's body to my car, putting her in the trunk.

# Chapter 8

## Barbie Bennett

Benz had better be glad that I fell asleep when he hung up on me. Them damn pain pills knocked my ass out. I thought I was cool at first. I was about to get out of bed, and as far as I made it was pulling the cover back. I woke up with Benz's nieces all over the bed. One had her feet in my face. The other one had her feet in my ass. To make matters worse, I was freezing my ass off. I fell asleep with a tank and undies on.

Opening my eyes, I stretched, and looked around. The girls weren't in bed with me anymore. I assumed that they went downstairs to eat breakfast with my parents. I was glad they weren't in the room because I was about to cuss Benz's black ass out. I called him. No answer. I called this nicca again. No answer. So, I sent his ass a nasty ass text.

**Me: You got a lot of nerve proposing to me, and you're entertaining the next bitch all night. Who the fuck do you think I am? A fool? I think not. I love your ass, but not that**

**much. You must think I'm crazy to sit over here and still be ready to marry your ass after you're fucking around with someone else. I know that's why you didn't answer. You're probably laid up with that hoe, feeding her the same lies that you fed me. You got me fucked up. I will not only beat your ass, but I'm going to put hands on her sorry ass too**.

I stopped texting for a moment, thinking that maybe he was going to call me back or at least text. When that nicca didn't say shit, I went in on his ass again.

**Me: You know what? I never should have said yes to you. Your ass is a dog. I knew that, but I thought that what we had was so special that maybe you would change for me. That's what all the stupid ass books say. They keep saying that a man that truly loves you and is meant to be yours will change for you. I thought that's what you were doing when you proposed. Then again, I should have known. Once a dog, always a dog.**

When Benz didn't text me back this time, I just spazzed. I went in on his ass. I called him every name in the book. I even went low saying shit that I knew would get under his skin. I was certain that he would call me back after I sent this text. Moments went by, no reply. I was fuming. After tossing my phone on the bed, I took a shower, dressed, and raced downstairs to breakfast with everyone else. All the kids were sitting quietly, eating. My father was reading the paper, and my mother was watching

*Sesame Street* with the kids.

"Hey, Ma. Hey, Dad."

They both spoke as I fixed my plate and sat down by the girls.

"What do you two have planned today?'

"Nothing much," my mother said. "The kids and I are going to go to the store after breakfast."

"I'm watching the game that I fell asleep on last night," my father commented.

"What are you doing?" my mother asked me."

"I'm going over to check on Benz. He just moved back into his place."

"I assume. I haven't seen it after the fire. I'm going back over there to see."

My phone dinged, and I almost jumped out of my skin.

"I think this is Benz. Toodles."

I got up and practically tripped over my own feet trying to get out of the kitchen. Racing upstairs, I barely got into my room before I checked my text. As soon as I closed the door, my phone dinged again before I could check the message. Then, it was ringing. I didn't even bother to look at the screen when I answered.

"Bitch!" Corset screamed on my FaceTime. "The fuck did Benz do for you to send me this damn email?"

My eyes bucked, and I scrolled through my text messages

and realized that I didn't email my last rant to Benz. It went to Corset. I was so embarrassed.

"My bad, cuzo. I thought I sent that to Benz. And it was a text, not an email."

"Shit as long as you wrote the damn thing, I couldn't tell the difference."

I fell back on the bed, laughing. It wasn't a funny situation, but the look on Corset's face was priceless. It was a mix of confused and pissed. Clearly, she didn't know what was going on with me, and I was too tickled in the moment to express it to her. Once I got all the giggles out of me, I addressed the subject.

"Benz pissed me the hell off. I'm sorry I took it out on you."

"What did he do?"

"He moved back into his home and didn't tell me. He's gone wait until I'm at my parent's house to do some underhanded shit like that. Then on top of it, he had a bitch over there."

"Oh, we need to pop up over there. I'm ready to cut that hoe's eyes out."

"Well, that's where I was going before you called. I actually thought you was Benz."

Corset rolled her eyes to the sky and back. "What did that nicca do? He called off the proposal, didn't he?"

"No."

"He accidentally sent you a picture of another hoe?"

"No. Not actually."

"Wait. Don't tell me that this nicca got another bitch pregnant? I'ma kill him."

"No, girl, calm down, Nothing like that. I was talking to him, and I thought I heard a bitch in the background. Then, the phone went dead. I tried to call him back. I texted him a million times, and I still haven't heard from him."

Corset twisted her face up. "Is that it? You have to be kidding me. You're overreacting. Cake hasn't hit me back in a minute. I've called texted and left message after message. This nicca ain't thought about my ass. I feel like something is wrong. That's what my spirit says, but in the back of my mind, I feel like he's run away with some hoe. I can't shake the feeling though."

"Are you sure? You two aren't together, you know. That open relationship bullshit or friends with benefits mess. Whatever you two call it. Maybe, he's moved on."

"I don't think so. Cake and I might be in a situatioship, but we talked frequently. The fact that he isn't answering my calls is a red flag. Even if he dodges them other bitches, he always talks to me. This ain't like Cake."

"Listen, cousin, I hate to tell you, but Cake might be the enemy."

"I don't believe that," she disputed.

62

"Well, according to Benz, Cake shot Malice. His words, not mine."

"I'm not sure what happened, but I know Cake very well. He would never shoot either one of them. He loves Benz and Malice despite his cocky ass attitude. We've talked many times. I just think that he's misunderstood. He's jealous of their brotherly bond, but he would never hurt them."

"You might be right, but Benz said Malice mentioned his name when he asked who shot him."

"Something's not right. Even if he was at odds with Benz and Malice, he would have answered my calls. In our last conversation, we talked about making things official."

"Hmmm. That's deep. Are you ready for that?"

"I don't know. I told him to let me think about it, and I haven't heard from him since. In fact, nobody has heard from him."

"That is strange. I'll tell Benz. Not sure how he's going to react. He's certain that Cake is the enemy."

"That's cuzo. Tell me what he says."

"Aight."

### *•.¸♡ Barbie & Benz ♡¸.•*

As I pulled up and parked in front of my condo, I noticed there was a car parked in front of Benz's place. See, this was that bullshit that I wasn't about to put up with. I reached into the

63

secret compartment in my car where Benz kept his gun, retrieved it, and got the fuck out. Somebody was about to die today.

Instead of going in through the front door, I used my key and went through the back. I wanted to catch this nicca in the act. Walking inside, I noticed how different his place looked. It was really nice. Too bad I was about to fuck it up. I held the gun by my side as I walked from the kitchen to the living room. I checked all the rooms downstairs including the basement before I proceeded upstairs.

I sauntered into the spare bedroom first. I guess a part of me was scared to see who might be in Benz's bedroom. I even checked the upstairs bathroom before standing in front of his closed bedroom door. I turned the doorknob, and the shit was locked. Without thinking twice, I raised the gun and shot the lock off, rushing inside.

Benz jumped out of bed with his gun pointed at me. I could tell he was about to pull the trigger until he realized it was me.

"Barbie, dammit, the fuck is wrong with you? I almost shot your crazy ass."

Benz sighed and lowered his gun as if everything was all good. I was still upset. I was determined to find this bitch that he was hiding.

"Where's the bitch at?"

"What?" Benz asked me, looking confused as ever.

I didn't even wait for him to answer. Yanking the closet

door open I looked inside. Then, I went into his bathroom, pulling back the curtain, looking in the bathroom closet, and under the sink."

"Do you really think a bitch could fit under the sink?" Benz asked, looking at me like I'd lost all the good sense God gave me.

"You're right. The hoe is under the bed."

Benz watched me as I stooped down, looking under the bed, smirking. I stood up out of breath after I didn't find a woman under the bed.

"Are you satisfied, Trigger?" His eyes lowered to the gun that I was still holding.

"You think you're cute, don't you?"

Benz walked up on me, taking the gun away from me, and sat it down on the dresser. Holding me by the hand, he led me over to the bed, massaging my shoulders.

"You came in my crib, acting a whole fool, blowing my bedroom door off the hinges, and shit. I just got my damn crib back, and here your black ass come, tearing shit up. As you can see ain't no bitch up in here. It's just me."

"Well how was I supposed to know that? You were acting funny last night and then you just hung up on me. I assumed that because you moved back into your place you were back to your old ways."

"What makes you think that I would cheat on you after I

asked you to marry me? That's just plain ole stupid. Give me more credit than that, Barbie."

"You're right. I let my thoughts get the best of me. I'm sorry."

Benz stopped massaging my shoulders. He grabbed his phone, typed the in something, and all of a sudden, I heard *You by Jaquees*. Kneeling before me, he took off my shoes and socks and started massaging my feet.

*I feel like I should be your lover, I should be your friend*
*All those silly issues made up in your head*
*Money can pay for your time but it's not love (Yeah)*
*And love cannot pay for that shit that I bought ya*
*Swear to god I should be gone and leave you alone, 'cause I*

"I know what you're trying to do," I exclaimed. "I'm not giving you none."

"Shhhh," Benz advised, kissing my feet in between massaging them.

*Rather be with you and all your bullshit*
*Rather be with you and all your bullshit*
*I'd rather be with you and all your bullshit*
*Rather be with you and all your bull*
*You (Yeah babe)*
*You (Ooh Ooh yeah)*
*You, yeah*
    *This is what I don't get*
*Don't know why I'm still here*
*All my passwords reset, yeah*
*And I know you did that shit*

I was so turned on. He knew that rubbing my feet was a sweet spot. I bit my lip so that I didn't let out a soft moan. I didn't stop Benz when he pulled down my jeans and removed my top. I was braless so my harden nipples were exposed. Benz held my breasts in his hands licking and sucking them both like Thanksgiving dinner.

"Is that pussy wet for me yet?"

I swallowed hard and nodded my head. I was so hot that I couldn't speak. My pussy was wet and tingling by the time Benz pulled my panties down my thighs.

"Take your time. The bleeding has stopped, but I still have slight pain."

"I'll take it easy on you. This time," I winked.

Lightly pushing me back on the bed, he pushed my legs back, cupping my ass, planting his face right in the middle. His tongue swirled around my plump vagina, licking the outer folds before he focused on the creamy center. With sensual flicks of his tongue he made love to my clit before sticking his fingers inside of me.

After while, I was slamming my box into his face. Having my legs so far back allowed my clit to be exposed. The warmness from his mouth and the cool air from the room had me on a rollercoaster. My climax was building. I was climbing the steep attraction before I got to the top and fell at a ferocious speed. The feeling was so incredible. I wanted to hold on to it forever, but I couldn't. I lost it. Squirting my juices. Not once, not twice, but four times.

"I guess someone was backed up too."

I giggled and covered my face.

"Don't be shy now. Keep the legs open so I can feel every inch of this juicy pussy."

Benz stepped out of his boxers, stroking his massive hard on. His weight rested on the bed as he rubbed his thick erection up and down my sticky honey pot. Promptly, he slid himself inside of me. I wrapped my legs around him tightly, moaning like crazy. I was trying my hardest not to yell. I didn't want him to know that I was whipped.

"Arrgh!" Benz grunted. "Damn. I almost forgot what this pussy felt like. It's been too long."

"Oh. Oh. Yes. It. Has."

I wanted to let out a few more moans, but my body wasn't having it. My orgasm ripped through my body, and I gushed all over Benz and the bed.

"Man, I love this pussy."

Benz was still stroking me as I felt mini orgasms dancing between my legs. I laid on the bed too tired to climax anymore, so I just let my body do it's thing. Benz made the ugliest face ever. I thought he was going to turn into an alien and fly away. His eyes went into the back of his head and his body convulsed like a zombie. If I wasn't so tired, I might have pushed his horror story looking ass off of me and run for the hills. Benz howled and then dumped loads of cum inside of me. I was still dripping when he went soft and rolled over on his back next to me.

"That was amazing. Give me like eight minutes and I'll be ready for round two."

"Oh no, I'm not. I slipped up this time, but you won't be getting no more of this nookie until our wedding night."

"You really meant that shit? I thought you were just talking like usual."

"Nope. I really meant it. After worrying if you were with another chick all night, I need some reassurance."

"I gave you a ring. And after you plan the wedding, I'm going to give you my last name and half of my bank account. We have to hold off on sex too?"

"Yes. We do. You've never waited for sex a day in your life. If you want a commitment from me, you have to commit to everything, including giving up something to prove yourself to me."

"Why can't I give up my car instead? I'd rather catch the bus than to give up pussy. That's cruel punishment. I ain't gone be able to do it."

"You better if you want to walk down the aisle with me. Marriage is a big deal. If you can't give up something so minor for ninety days then I guess we're not meant to be."

# Princess Diamond

Benz slapped his forehead with his hand. "You got less than ninety days to plan this wedding. I'll be lucky if my dick still works by the time we go on our honeymoon."

"Am I not worth it?" I asked, batting my long eyelashes.

Benz rolled over on his side, facing me. "Nah, not really."

Benz laughed and I smacked his ass with a pillow. "Your ass better walk through fire for me, nicca."

He kissed my cheek. "After almost losing you, I look forward to being your husband. Even if that means I have to get blue balls to do so."

I laughed and snuggled next to him.

"Blue is your favorite color," I chided.

Benz groaned and scooted away from me.

# Chapter 9

## Brysen "Benz" Sorensen

"Everything good?"

"Yeah. Sort of," my street lieutenant said.

Him and his crew had been taking care of things since Cake went missing and Malice got shot.

"Aw fuck. What's that supposed to mean? Shit ain't good?"

"It's good, for now. I'm just worried about later."

"Stop speaking in circles. What the fuck are you hinting at?"

"I didn't want to bother you, but we're almost out of product."

I had to think about what he said. "Fuck!" Cake always handled this shit, but now I have to because this nicca had disappeared.

"You good bro?"

"I'm good. Just keep handling business as usual."

"I'm on it," he said as I walked away from the trap.

I called Sabre, but I didn't get an answer, so I sent him a text. He hit me right back.

**Sab: Tied up bro, but I'm come check you later. I got something you want to hear.**

I knew what that meant. He has some serious information for me.

**Me: Cool. I'll be at the crib. Tec and I have a game to play.**

**Sab: Cool.**

Barbie was out doing the wedding thing with Corset, so I had some time to kill. Tec hit me up earlier and said he wanted to go live. I hadn't been on my channel playing in awhile. He had been doing features on my channel for me, but it was time that I showed my face once again. I wanted to throw a party, but shit was too hot in the streets for me right now.

When I got home, Tec was already there waiting on me.

"Sup, bro?"

Tec got out of his car with a huge grin. "Bro, you ready to kick some ass, bro?"

I chuckled. "It's been a minute. I only got a couple hours to play. Sab gonna slide through. When he gets here, I have business to handle."

"A couple of hours is all we need to go live and get paid now that we got millions of subscribers. I already put the word out that we were going to be on soon so they needed to stay tuned."

"Bet. We about to be lit."

Tec followed me into my spot, and we proceeded to the gaming room. It was everything a nicca could ask for when it comes to playing online. The décor was crazy. Blue, black, and green which beamed neon colors when I cut the lights off.

When I tell you that my gaming room was something serious, it was a major problem. I had the most hi-tech equipment ever. I'm talking life-size monitors with cameras surrounding the room so that we could be seen from every angle for YouTube, Twitch, and our    Patreon account. Cool gaming chairs, microphones, headsets, and anything else needed to pull off a litty ass live stream. One side of the room was life-sized. It was set up for us to play standing up. The other side of the room had the desktop set up with the powerhouse computer that helped us become champions.

Since we hadn't gone live in a minute, I decided to stand up and give the fans a show. I was playing in a robe, boxers, and weed socks on one side of the room flexing for my fans while Tec was sitting down at the desktop on the other side of the room, shirtless, showing off his pecs. We knew we were stunning to look at and niccas always hated on us for that. They called us every name under the sun, but the fact of the matter was no matter what they said, we could play our asses off. We were doing our thing. Acting a fool for the camera, winning left and right. It showed by the amount of donations that poured in. I was glad that we had an automatic thank you set up when people supported our channel because there was no way that we could have thanked them all individually and kicked ass in the game too.

I paused the game and turned around to Tec, pointing at the phone. He said he would continue to play the game live until it was over and then he would come join me. I nodded and left the room to go talk to Sabre.

"What up, Sab?" I asked, opening the door to let him in.

"I got a lot to say."

"Aight. Hang tight. Tec is finishing up a live. Once he gets off the phone. We can talk."

Sabre nodded and headed to the kitchen, grabbing a bag of my favorite chips.

"Nicca, you better put them back and get that other bag of chips. You know those are mine."

Sab looked me dead in the eye and opened the back, taking out a chip, biting it.

I snickered. "That's some disrespectful shit. Wait until I show up at your crib again. I'ma eat your shit too."

Sab smirked and continued to eat my damn Fritos. "You got some chili and cheese so I can hook them up."

"Hell no. I don't plan on your ass staying that long."

Sab chuckled, grabbed him a pop, and sat my kitchen

island. I stared his ass down. I was about to cuss his ass out when Tec walked in.

"Today had to be a record high for donations. I'll double check to see how much later."

We slapped it up and grinned. I'm sure he was smiling, thinking about the money we pulled in just like I was. Once Tec and I gathered ourselves from our gaming high, we took a seat at the island with Sabre.

"What's good, Sab?"

"What's good, Tec?"

"So, what did you have to tell me?"

Sabre licked his fingers and belched loudly.

"Gross muthafuckin' ass," I announced.

Sabre and Tec laughed.

"If I didn't want to know what you had to say so bad, I would toss your nasty ass out. Say excuse me."

Sabre belched again and grinned.

"Nicca say what you got to say so you can get your foul ass out my shit."

"All jokes aside. I got something important to tell you. I found out who hit you and Barbie that day."

"Who?" Tec and I both asked, sounding like two owls.

"That muthafucka Archie."

"Say what now?" Tec asked.

I shook my head. "I had a feeling it was that punk ass

muthafucka. I was just hoping that maybe it was really an accident. I don't care what Barbie said, that nicca is dead. I'm not about to sit back and wait for him to take me out."

I had been looking for this nicca anyway because I wanted to find out if he hired Dache to kill me. Surely, he had motive to do so. After what happened between him and Barbie, I was certain that he couldn't have been happy about our engagement.

"You got an address on this nicca?" I asked Sabre.

"Sure do."

"I know you been out of the game for a minute, but are you ready to put in some work?"

"Hell yeah," Sabre commented. "It'll be like I never left."

"What you need me to do?" Tec wondered. "I'm ready to ride out too."

"Stay here and play the game online. You know you always joke about pretending to be me?"

"Yeah. I got a mean impression of you."

"Cool. Do that shit and play online here at my crib until I get back. Don't show your face tho."

"I got you, bro. Impersonations is what I do."

Tec and I dapped it up and he went back to my gaming room. I left him with a gun just in case he needed it. Although, I had a whole gun room built into this mutha. It was a secret hidden room.

I changed into my black hoodie, black jeans, and black

boots. Sabre came prepared. He already knew what time it was. The nicca was already dressed in black. We jumped into Sabre's ride and rolled out.

Archie lived in the suburbs like I suspected. This bourgeois nicca stayed in a condo out in Tinley Park. He popped all that hot shit. I knew he was a pussy because he acted like one even though he tried to front like he wasn't. Just another lame ass black boy trying to be white.

Archie must've been going somewhere, probably trying to get away. Too bad for him. He opened the door carrying a shoulder bag and wheeling a suitcase. His eyes widened when he saw me and Sabre standing there about to knock on the door he just opened. I'm sure he knew why we were here, but he was too damn slow to react. I punched that nicca in the face as hard as I could. He fell back into the apartment on his ass. Sabre kicked his bags back into the apartment and closed the door. I looked that nicca in his eyes, and tased his ass.

While he was knocked out, we went through his place with gloves on of course and robbed this nicca blind. Anything he had of value belonged to us now. All the money he had stashed was ours, including the money he had on him. I'm assuming he just left the bank because the bills were nice and crisp, just the way I liked them.

After running this nicca's pockets, I drug his ass over to the couch and waited for his ass to wake the fuck up. Sabre and I were chilling in his living room looking at his ass when he woke up. I was on his couch and Sabre was by the door playing video games with the .44 on his lap. If Archie tried anything stupid, he was going to get popped from every angle.

As soon as his eyes opened, Sabre and I were ready to spring into action.

"Am I still alive?" Archie asked.

I plopped down on the couch next to him and slapped his face really hard. "The fuck you think? What kind of stupid ass question is that?"

"No question is a stupid question," he tried to reason.

I knew what his lame ass was trying to do. Throw me off my game so that I wouldn't see his next move coming.

"See, that's why you're in the predicament you're in right now. Doing lame ass shit."

Sabre chuckled. I could tell that he was just glad to be back in the mix. We've fucked up many of muthafuckas back in the day before he retired. Archie stood up as if he was actually going to leave, and I pushed his ass back down. This time, he fell into the chair. I walked around the chair like a shark circling its prey. The more I circled him, the more nervous Archie got.

"Tell me about your relationship with Barbie?" I quizzed as I stopped walking standing right in front of his low-life ass.

"Uh...um...There is nothing to tell."

"That's not what you said at the hospital, muthafucka. You

had a lot of shit to say so let's hear it."

"You misunderstood," Archie tried to deflect.

"Nah, nicca, I heard your punk ass just right. Keep that same energy as you did back then and pop that hot shit right now."

"I don't know what you're talking about?"

I punched his ass in the face to refresh his memory.

"Do you know now?"

That nicca looked at me crossed-eyed. If I wasn't in go mode I might have laughed.

"You're full of shit. What I want to know is what happened between you and Barbie?"

He hesitated and I revved my arm back about to punch that nicca in the face once again.

"Okay. Okay. I'll tell you," his pussy ass conceded. "That night. She was so drunk. I didn't want to take her home like that, so I got a hotel room. I helped her inside, and she staggered over to the bed. She kept complaining that it was hot, and I couldn't figure out the air conditioner, so she started stripping. She passed out on the bed and I slept in the chair. That was that. I lied about the whole thing."

I paced back and forth. "Nah, bruh, that shit don't make no sense. Why was she so hot? Barbie and I have drank plenty of times and she never mentioned being hot." That's when the shit hit me like a light bulb illuminating. "Did you slip something in her drink? Is that why she was hot?"

Archie hung his head low so I already knew the answer but I wanted to hear his punk ass say it. "Yes. I just wanted her to loosen up and have a good time. That's all. I swear."

"No, muthafucka. You wanted her to fuck you so you decided to drug her, get a hotel room, and date rape her."

"No. No. I didn't."

Rage took over me and I had that nicca in a headlock before I could stop myself. I was going to choke his ass out right there, killing his stupid ass. With all of my might, I tried to break his neck. The choke hold I had on him was so strong. He didn't stand a chance. His eyes bulged and one more second later, he was going to be out this bitch. When I let him go, he coughed as spit spewed from his mouth.

I looked over at Sabre who was done with the game on his phone. I nodded and he knew what time it was. We both put the small electronic device in our mouth to disguise our voices. I didn't like using these things, but as we were searching his place, I got a feeling that it was bugged. Although, Sabre swept the place clean, he didn't find any cameras, but that didn't mean there wasn't a wire somewhere. After all, this nicca was suspect like a muthafucka. I wouldn't put it passed him. If anyone could be a snitch, it would be this lame ass nicca.

Since we didn't trust Archie or his apartment, we pretended as if we were going to leave. The dumb nicca actually thought we were going to let him make it. He gathered his things and left his apartment about to make a clean get away. Before he could get in his car, I put a pillowcase over his face while Sabre took his keys and put his suitcases into the trunk of his car. Sabre pulled off in his ride while I stuffed that nicca into Sabre's trunk. While Sabre made Archie's ride disappear, I was going to make Archie disappear.

"You thought you were hot shit because Barbie paid you a little bit of attention, didn't you?"

"No," Archie said, squirming. He was tied to a chair at one of my warehouses so I could speak freely and do as I pleased.

"You're on my turf now, nicca. Shit's about to get muthafuckin' real."

"Wha-what do you plan to do?" Archie stammered. "I didn't do nothing to Barbie. Everything was a lie."

I raised my gun and shot him in the knee cap. He screamed like a bitch.

"That's the problem Archie. You lied and I hate a fuckin' liar."

I raised my gun again and shot him in his other knee cap. He screamed even louder this time, but I didn't give a fuck.

"I tried to let the bullshit you did slide, but I couldn't. You drugged my chick and then you had raped her."

"No. No. I didn't. I lied about that. I swear. I didn't have sex with Barbie. I mean, I wanted to, but I didn't. I couldn't. I just couldn't do her like that."

"Did you get a conscious before or after you drugged her?"

Archie looked from the gun I was holding to me and whimpered. "After."

"Wrong answer."

I raised my gun and shot his ass in his left shoulder. He hollered in pain once again, and this time I laughed.

"What about the baby? Did you lie about that too?"

I already knew the answer, but I wanted this bastard to confirm it. Call it an ego trip if you want to, but I was loving every minute of this shit. I've been waiting a long time to bust Archie's balls. This was a dream come true.

"It was a lie, man. I swear. I never touched Barbie," Archie pleaded. "I just wanted to get back at you when I found out she was pregnant. I loved her, but she didn't love me back the way she loved you."

"Damn right," I boasted.

"Don't kill me. Please, I'll disappear and never bother you or Barbie again. Just let me go."

"I'm afraid I can't do that. You killed my seed."

"I promise, I didn't do it."

"So, you're saying you didn't ram your car into us, almost killing us?"

"No. Someone hit me over the head. I was passed out in the parking garage. When I came to myself, I was in the hospital. I have no idea what happened in between."

I chuckled. "Bullshit. Once a liar, always a liar."

"You have a point. I admit I did the other stuff, but I didn't hit you. I swear."

"So, you didn't send anyone to kill me at my condo either?"

"What?" he questioned. "No. Of course not."

"I find that hard to believe."

"I don't know what else to tell you, man. I confessed to what I did. All that other stuff, it wasn't me."

"Too little too late. The fact that you drugged Barbie and thought about date rape was enough to seal your fate in hell."

I popped him in the other shoulder as he continued to plead for his life. When I got tired of hearing him beg, I put him out of his misery with a bullet between his eyes.

Immediately, I called Traffik and told him and his crew to sweep his place to see if it was bugged. Even though we checked it out, we couldn't be too sure. Then, I told them to meet me here at the warehouse to dispose of Archie's dead body.

As I waited, I couldn't help but to replay in my mind what Archie said. He confessed to everything, but the hit and run, and Dache showing up to kill me. The more I thought about it, the more it didn't make any sense. He had a point. Why tell the truth about some and not it all?

I pulled out my phone and texted the lil homie Kapri. He

said if I ever need a favor to hit him up. If there was ever a time, it was now. I needed to know the truth. Did I just kill an innocent man? Well, let me rephrase that. He wasn't innocent. He intended to do wrong, he just didn't get a chance too. However, I still wanted to know the truth because if he wasn't the one who hit me, then who did? And if he wasn't the one who sent Dache to kill me, then who did? I thought killing Archie was going to solve everything. Now, it seems as if everything I thought I knew was just a hoax. I was back where I fuckin' started with this bullshit.

# Chapter 10

## Brysen "Benz" Sorensen

I was cuddled up with Barbie on the couch at her spot. Even though I lived next door, she wanted to do the whole dating thing until we got married. So like in the past, sometimes we were at her spot, sometimes we were at mine, and sometimes we had alone time.

At first, I was kind of shitty about this arrangement. First, she said no sex. Then, I couldn't see my girl everyday either. I was ready to call this whole thing off. Once I thought about it more, I realized that absence does make the heart grow fonder. We were getting along better, missing each other more, and appreciating our quality time. Between my street shit and her wedding planning, we barely had time to see each other, which made things sweeter when we did.

"How is the wedding planning going?"

Barbie lifted her head off my shoulder. "Not so good. Corset and I are tired trying to figure this all out.

"You mean to tell me between you and all your cousins, y'all can't figure none of this girlie shit out?"

"Xstaci helped me, but as you know she lives in New York. There's only so much FaceTime that's going to help me."

"Listen babe don't stress yourself. I don't care if you showed up in jeans and at raggedy ass shirt, I'm going to marry you regardless."

What did I say that for? Barbie gave me the angriest look ever. You would have thought that I smacked her upside her head or something.

"Are you serious?" he asked with a nasty tone.

"Yes. I'm serious. I'm not marrying you because you're in a fancy ass dress, or because we're in an expensive venue, or a three-tier cake. That's all for show. The only thing I'm concerned about is giving you my last name and making you my wife. The rest of that bullshit is to impress other people. If it were left up to me we would go to the Justice of Peace or elope and be done with all this mess. A destination wedding sounds good to me."

Barbie stared me down with her mouth wide open.

"Fuck it. No matter what I say, I'm not going to win this shit. I'll check on you later."

I got my ass up and left before she cussed me out for some shit that I didn't even understand. Why were women so complicated? I was confessing that I loved her no matter what and she was looking at me like I had a dick growing out of my forehead.

I jumped in my ride. I needed to cool off, so I decided to take a little drive. I wasn't going anywhere particular. Just rolling through the streets in my all blue with the blue interior trimmed in black Lamborghini Urus. I pulled this big boy out when I was trying to shit on niccas. Not only was it an attention grabber, it rode smooth as fuck.

I was bumping my favorite rapper Key Glock, riding slow through the streets when I seen a nicca that I used to fuck with. He used to cop product from me. He was a slime ball. The nicca claimed my prices were too high, so he was going to start copping from his cousin. Instead of beating that nicca's ass, I just cut him off. I knew he was lying, but I cut my losses and kept it moving. I was going to let that nicca make it until I noticed he was wearing a Rolex.

Everyone knew damn well that he was a small-time hustler. He didn't make enough to rock a Rolex. I lost one that looked just like it a couple months back. A blue and gold vintage Rolex. I almost didn't see it. This nicca was flossing, being over dramatic and shit. His hands all in the air and the sun was hitting my hundred-thousand dollar watch just right. I asked this nicca a few times if he had my shit and he lied each time saying that he didn't have it. Nicca told me someone else stole it. He dropped a name and everything. Now, I'm thinking I probably popped the wrong nicca for stealing my shit. Then again, hat nicca that I popped was a low life too. If I didn't take his ass out, somebody else would have. Indirectly, I did the city a favor by killing his slime ball ass.

I whipped my ride around in the middle of the street and ran that bitch up on the sidewalk, jumping out with my gun in my hand. I knew what I was doing was risky, but I didn't give a fuck. This nicca needed to be taught a lesson. The dudes talking to Plunky scattered like roaches. They moved so fast, I didn't see which way them niccas went. Before Plunky could run off, I had my Glock pointed at that nicca's head.

"Muthafucka run me my watch."

"Yo, Benz, what you talking about?" this nicca lied.

I didn't have anymore patience for his low life ass. Losing my temper, I popped that nicca right in the foot. He started hopping, holding his wounded foot until he fell. I stood over his ass, snatching my watch off his wrist.

"Now run them fuckin' pockets too."

"Damn. You already took my watch. You gone take my money too."

I waved the gun in his face. "That's my money now, nicca. That's interest for letting your broke ass babysit my watch."

I looked around and noticed that people were starting to gather.

"You're lucky, bitch."

I jogged back to my truck, jumping in and speeding off. What I did was reckless, so I had to do damage control. I hit up Traffik and told him to handle the people in that area, letting them know to keep their mouths shut. I also sent him a code to dead Plucky's stupid ass. I knew that as soon as he could tell, he was going to rat my ass out so he had to die. I had to hit up Sabre and tell him what the fuck just happened.

"Yo, Sab. Guess who the fuck I just ran down on?"

"Aw fuck. Who?"

"That nicca Plucky."

"I thought that nicca was dead."

"Nah, he's still alive. Well, not for long."

"What that nicca do?"

"You remember my Vintage Rollie? The one that went missing?"

"Yep. I was the nicca helping you look for it. How could I forget?"

"It was on this nicca Plucky's wrist."

"Fuck outta here," Sabre said in disbelief.

"Nah, bro. Real shit. This nicca was on the corner flashing my shit like it was his. Then he had the nerve to lie. I swooped down on his ass so fast, he ain't know what hit him. After I popped that nicca, I took my watch back and ran that nicca's pockets."

"How much you get?"

"Just a rack but fuck it. Money is money. That nicca ain't gone need it in the dirt."

"Fuck him. Where you at now?"

"Riding down 95th. Why?"

"Come scoop me. I want to see Malice."

"Cool. I was going to visit him anyway. You might as well come too."

Seventeen minutes later, I was at Sabre's house, picking him up.

"I see you on your petty shit riding around in the Lambo. This muthafucka is hard though."

"I know it is. Pick up your mouth, nicca."

Sabre flipped me the finger. "Fuck you, nicca."

I chuckled and popped the locks.

As Sabre got in my whip, Rozi was in the doorway. "Don't be getting my husband in trouble, Benz. You know he's retired. I don't want him on that street bullshit like you."

"Why don't you yell it louder so the rest of the block can hear you?" I asked snidely. She knew better than to say that shit out loud like that. Big ass mouth.

"I don't give a fuck, Benz. Don't make me have to find you."

"Aight, Rozi," I said so she would shut the fuck up.

"Bye, baby," Sabre said as I pulled off.

"Damn, you need to keep your wife in line. She gone blow

up my damn spot. I thought you schooled her."

"First off, don't be talking about my wife."

"Then silence her ass unless you want us both to be sitting in a cell."

Sabre nodded. He didn't say another word about his wife because he knew I was telling the truth. That's how niccas got jammed up, cause of a running mouth ass bitch. I handed Sabre a blunt. By the look on his face, he needed that shit.

"How's lil man doing?" I asked, referring to his son.

"He's good. Getting big. I can't believe he's in first grade already."

"Wow. That's crazy. I remember when he was born."

"Me too. I want another one before Junior gets too old."

"I feel you. I was glad I had a brother close to my age. Malice and I were besties growing up."

Just the mention of my brother's name made me feel some type of way. I've been keeping my thoughts about how I really felt to myself. I didn't want to breakdown. I had to be strong for him. Although, they didn't see much improvement in his status, I truly believed that he was going to wake up any moment. Silently, I prayed in my head whenever someone mentioned Malice's name. I couldn't imagine living without him so he had to make it.

My phone rang. It was the lil homie.

"Yo, what's good, bro?"

"Everything is everything," Kapri said.

"I got you on speaker. Did you get that news for me?"

"Indeed. Where you at? I'ma pull up and speak that shit in person."

"Cool."

I shared my location with him and sat my phone back in the cup holder.

"Who was that?"

"My lil homie. He's young, but he's on point. I asked him to look into Archie for me."

"Why you looking into that nicca? If he's dead, let it be."

"Nah, bro. He said some shit that got me to thinking."

"I know you didn't grow a conscience after deading his ass."

"It ain't like that Sab. Shit just didn't add up, so I hit Kapri up. I just need to make sure that it isn't another enemy out here lurkin' on my ass, and I end up being a sitting duck."

"I get it. Hopefully, that nicca was lying about whatever he said and we can get back to business as usual."

"I wish it were that easy. I still don't know where Cake is. That shit don't make no sense either. He's a hard-headed ass stubborn muthafucka, but I still can't wrap my head around the fact that he shot Malice and disappeared."

"I agree. That's some foul shit. Why don't you get your lil homie to find Cake?"

"I'm trying to give that nicca a chance to come to me like a man. If he don't show up soon, I'm going to go looking for him. That's not what he wants. I won't be as understanding if I have to look for him. Right now, I just want to paralyze the nicca or fucked him up. If he stays in hiding too long, I'm going to pop his ass and be done with it. My aunt will just be minus another son."

"I forgot Cake's brother was killed."

"That's why I'm trying not to take this nicca's life. I don't want to hurt my aunt by suffering the loss of another child."

As Sabre and I were talking, we saw Kapri ride right pass us in a silver Bugatti.

"There's that little nicca right there."

"He's riding hard in that Bugatti. He looks like one of them Diaz-Santana niccas."

"I believe he is."

"How did you link up with him? That family don't usually fuck with outsiders."

"The Jakes towed both of our cars and we kinda bonded over that moment. It's more to it, but that's how we met."

Kapri got out of his ride, pulling up his pants. He was a fresh little nicca. I honked the horn and he looked in our direction and started walking our way. Sabre and I got out of the car, meeting him halfway. Kapri stopped and pulled out what appeared to be a cellphone, but when he opened it, I could tell it wasn't.

"What's that?" I asked curiously.

"It's a device to scramble our conversation. I don't want anyone nearby to hear what we have to say."

Sabre and I looked at each other. We were both impressed. Kapri looked at Sabre and I could tell that he was hesitant because he didn't know him.

"Kapri this is my boy, Sabre. He's family. Whatever you have to say, you can say it in front of him."

"Is that your real name?" Kapri asked.

"Yeah," Sabre admitted.

"What's your last name?"

Sabre looked at me sideways. I nodded and he answered while gritting his teeth. "Peoples."

Kapri nodded. He tucked the first gadget into his pocket and pulled out his phone. After texting for a hot second, he closed the phone, about to speak.

"Did you just check me out?" Sabre asked offended.

"I sure did. I don't know you, bro. No offense, but I don't fuck with just anybody."

Kapri's comment had me curious. "Did you run me too?"

"Yep. Sure did. I had to know who I was dealing with. I see that you're both real niccas, so we can proceed."

Sabre looked unimpressed with how smooth Kapri moved, but I was actually surprised. He was very knowledgeable to be so young. His moves were calculated. He didn't seem as reckless as most young men in the game.

Kapri sensed the tension and broke the silence by telling me what I needed to know. "Um, that Archie dude. He's all fake, yo. That nicca's real name is Eddie Green. Two crackhead parents, a little sister, and brother. He went to jail and ended up getting a plea deal, so he didn't have to do any time. Word on the street is he's the op, snitching and reporting to law enforcement for a while now. I'm not sure what happened to dude, but I hope you were watching your back the whole time, if you get my drift. I'm certain that if he wasn't wearing a wire, his house might have been bugged."

"Fuck!" I spat. "I knew it. Something was off about that muthafucka from jump."

While we were standing there chatting, a car that looked like Cake's slowed down.

"You know this nicca?" Kapri asked with his gun already drawn.

"I think it's my cousin's ride. I'm not sure tho."

As I squinted, trying to get a better look, the window rolled down just a little. I knew was going to happen next, but I was slow to react. Someone pointed a gun out of the window, blasting at us. The shit happened at lightning speed. The unknown person let of like six shots real quick and sped off.

Kapri was a real G because he kicked into high gear,

shooting back at them niccas, hitting the car with bullets as they sped down the street. I pulled out my piece, letting bullets fly too. I knew niccas were ruthless but damn. These niccas were grimy as fuck. They let off shots in broad daylight in front of a hospital. My mind flashed back to my cousin Cake. I couldn't shake the feeling that he was somehow involved. That shit had me heated. I guess I couldn't wait for him to show his face anymore. It was time to find him and dead this whole situation.

"Damn. The fuck are y'all into?" Kapri wondered.

We were both still on guard, looking around while glancing down the street. I don't know how Kapri felt, but I felt enraged. That was some sneak shit. Kapri and I were talking about the incident when medical staff came rushing out of the hospital towards us.

"I'll be in touch, yo," Kapri whispered in my ear. He snatched my gun before I could protest, walking backwards.

Kapri give me a head nod and scurried off. I knew why. He was saving both our ass from jail time when the police showed up. I was glad he had my back. That's something I would cherish for the rest of my life. Lil homie was the real deal. I was about to walk off when I noticed Sabre wasn't standing on the other side of me. He had fallen between two cars. He was on the ground, leaking blood. He had been hit at least four times. My heart dropped when I saw him gasping for air.

"Fuck!" I yelled.

I felt horrible. I just knew he was standing here talking with Kapri and I. The shit happened so fast we didn't know what had hit us, literally. Sabre came out of retirement for me. If he died, I would never forgive myself.

# Chapter 11

## Cailen "Caked Up" Sorensen

The day started off normal. I had no idea that before the day ended my cousin would be shot, and I would end up on the missing person's list. So, how did all of this bullshit start? Well, Malice and I were going to meet up with one of our regular clients. He ordered a lot of product because he moved weight too, so we always did the drop in pairs.

We'd been doing business with him for a hot minute, so shit was supposed to be all good. At least that's what we thought. Dealing with the street on a regular, I should have known to expect the unexpected.

Malice was driving and I was riding shotgun. I was talking shit as usual. We were smoking weed and chilling, bumping that old school rap. It was a whole vibe in the car. I got some things off my chest. He got some things off his.

"Have you talked to Benz," he asked.

"Nope," I answered, nonchalantly. "Was I supposed to?" I

asked with an attitude.

"C'mon, bro. Y'all need to squash this shit."

"What? I know you're not asking me to do it. He pulled a gun out on me first. I just returned the favor."

"You know how Benz is. That's why I'm asking you to be the bigger person."

"Nah, fuck that. It won't happen this time. He went too far. I understand that he's running shit. Hell, the whole world can see that he's running shit, but what he ain't running is me."

"This feud between you two has to stop. We're brothers."

"No," I corrected. "You two are brothers. I'm an outsider."

"Cake, you know I think of you as a brother."

"You might, but Benz doesn't. He gives me his ass to kiss every chance he gets. Like I told you before, when you need me, I'm always available. How available is that nicca when you call?"

Malice sighed. "I hate being stuck in the middle of this shit."

"Well get used to it. That's how it's gotta be until Benz realizes that he's not in this street shit alone. Until then, I'm not speaking to his ego trippin' ass."

Malice sighed again and I started laughing. "Being married has made your ass soft. You over there sighing like a little bitch."

Malice laughed. "It takes a bitch to know a bitch."

I started laughing too. That's how I knew we were both high as fuck because those would have been fighting words, and there we were, laughing our asses off like the shit was the funniest thing on earth.

We pulled up to the abandoned office building. This is where we usually meet, so I didn't think anything suspicious would pop off. As usual, I got my three guns. I tucked one in my waist and the other one in my ankle holder. Malice did the same thing before we looked around, got out, and went to the trunk to get the product. This particular client sold his shit out in the West Suburbs, so what he did out there didn't affect our business. That's all we cared about anyway.

Per usual, Malice held the duffle bag with the product in one hand and his gun in the other. Meanwhile, I tapped on the door with one hand while I held my third gun in my other hand. After banging on the door with our secret knock, I heard the locks being removed. When the door opened, I expected to see the client, but instead, I was greeted by a nicca I ain't never seen before.

Immediately, I knew something was up. I didn't wait for my instincts to prove that I was right before I popped the nicca in the head. That's when I saw more niccas behind him holding guns. Malice backed up going back to the car with the product. I was right behind him, but since I was closer to the door, I had to shoot at them niccas so that I could get the drop on them before they got the drop on me.

When the bullets started hailing from every direction, including hitting Malice's car, I made eye contact with him, giving him the nod leave me behind. I could tell that he didn't want to, but he had a wife and kids to think about. They needed him. I always told him that if it came down to his life or mine, I would take the fall because his family came first. I was single doing me. Therefore, I only had me to think about. He was a great father and an even better husband. Black love was where it was at. There was no way I would allow him to risk his life to save me.

I picked ole dude up that I shot in the dome and used him as a human shield until I could get behind a dumpster close by. I took cover behind it, shooting as many of those niccas as I could. They riddled Malice's car with a ton of bullets. It looked like they had hit Malice. If they did, he kept on driving like a real gangsta, getting away with the product. I didn't know if I was going to survive this shit or not, but if I was going to die, I was going to take as many of them niccas with me as I could. I pulled out my second gun and shot as many of them as I could.

It seemed like as many as I killed, more were steadily coming. There was no way I was going to outshoot them. I didn't want to punk out, but I had to. Dropping the dead body, I took off down the alleyway as fast as I could. I thought I was making progress until I got to the end of the alley and saw a car ride up. I felt just like Ricky did in *Boyz In The Hood*. In slow motion, I turned around and ran back towards the abandoned office. Not only was I running towards the niccas who were shooting at me, I had a car speeding down the alley trying to kill my ass at the same time.

I felt several shots hit me. I was lucky that I was wearing body armor. However, that didn't stop them from whipping my ass. All those bullets that I fired and that were fired at me, only pissed them off even more. I was back at the same door that I just tapped on because the alley was a dead end and they had me cornered. Once the car stopped and two people got out, I was surrounded. I just knew this was the end. I thought they were going to unload a million bullets on my ass.

Instead, they did something equally as bad. They jumped me. Kicking me all over my body until I passed out. I wasn't sure if I was dying, but I sure felt like it when they drug me into the abandoned office building.

# Chapter 12

## Brysen "Benz" Sorensen

I was back in the waiting room once again. I felt like no matter how much I tried to leave the gotdamn hospital, shit just kept on pulling me back. Rozi came stomping into the emergency room. She was the last person I wanted to see. I knew she was going to go in on my ass.

"You muthafucka!" Rozi yelled, punching at me wildly. "You said you would protect him. You promised."

"I know. I tried. Believed me, I did. Shit just got out of hand"

She punched my chest for a few more minutes and then collapsed in my arms. "You're going to have to bury both of us if Sabre dies. I can't live without him."

I held her close, comforting her in her time of need. "I know, but I don't even want to think like that. He's going to be okay. I believe that and you have to believe that."

"He better," Rozi screamed. "Otherwise, I'm going to kill

you and Barbie."

"What does Barbie have to do with any of this? I;m the one who asked him to come out of retirement."

"True, but I went along with it because of my cousin. I trusted you. I trusted her. Now, I'm about to be a widow and a single mother, yet you two have each other."

"You're making it worse. You're acting like you gave up already. He's a fighter. He'll make it. I know it."

"Whatever. You just better hope Sab lives, or I'ma be your worst nightmare, nicca." Rozi started to walk away, but she turned around to face me again. "And don't even think about visiting my husband. You're not welcome.

I realized she was hurt, but gotdamn she was taking this too far. I felt like Sabre was going to be good. I had to believe that because I couldn't live with myself if he died. I was about to take a seat in the waiting room once again when a doctor came up to me.

"You're Malice's brother, correct?"

"Yes," I replied.

"I was just about to call you. Your brother is up and he's asking for you."

I almost jumped out of my skin. "Stop talking and lead the way."

I followed behind the doctor as he traveled through the hospital to Malice's room. When I walked inside, Malice was sitting up. His tubes had been removed, and he was drinking water. Behati was standing next to him, dabbing at her eyes. I'm sure she was just overjoyed that her husband was now awake. I greeted Behati with a hug and a kiss on the cheek.

"Can you give us a minute?" Malice asked his wife.

She smiled and kissed Malice on the lips before she stepped out of the room

"Bro, I've been praying every day and every night for this moment. How do you feel?"

"Good. The doctors said that I'm going to have to go through extensive rehab to walk again, but I don't care at least I'm alive."

"Do you want me to get a second opinion? They could be wrong."

Behati already got a second and a third opinion. The bullet caused quite a bit of damage. At least I have feeling in my legs. That's a blessing."

I sighed when he said that.

"Don't even trip. I'm just glad to take fresh air into my lungs. If I need to go to therapy in order to walk again, I'm going to do that shit and come out of this whole thing even better than before."

"I feel you," I chuckled. "If anyone can do it, it's you. You have always done everything you put your mind to."

"Fa sho. However, that's not what I wanted to talk to you

about."

"What is it?"

"It's Cake."

"Say no more. I know he shot you. We're looking for him as we speak."

"What? No. He didn't shoot me. In fact, he saved my life. After the niccas that Cake and I were going to make the drop with shot me, they took him."

"But you said his name when I asked you who shot him."

"Listen, bro, I was trying to tell you he's in danger. You have to find him."

"Fuck!" I hollered. "That was a while ago, Malice. Anything could have happened by now."

"It could have, but no matter what, you have to find him."

I held my head down in anger. I wished that I knew this information sooner. "I'll find him. Let me make a few phone calls regarding the matter."

The nurse was walking in as I was walking out. She had Malice's water and what looked like tea. As soon as I was out of ear shot, I called Kapri and ran down the whole scenario to him. He told me that he was already looking into it and he'd follow back up when he had a plan. I hung up and walked back inside of Malice's room, enjoying my brother's company. It was so good to see him awake and in such good spirits.

# Barbie & Benz 3

Kapri showed up at my warehouse with two other goons.

"Yo, we're here to help any way we can. This is Bandz and Sir. They are new to the squad, but they are beasts in these streets."

I gave a nod to Sir, but when I locked eyes with Bandz, I realized that we knew each other from way back.

"What's up?" I greeted Bandz with a grin

He grinned and gave me a one-arm hug. "Good to see you, bruh."

"Likewise."

"I'm glad you two know each other," Kapri stated. "That'll make the job much easier. Everyone here is family and that's how we move."

"Y'all started without me," Tec announced, strolling in eating a hoagie.

Kapri, Bandz, and Sir pulled their guns fast as hell ready to blast my boy Tec away.

"Hol' up," I urged. "He's with me."

They all lowered their guns and welcomed him to the huddle.

"Okay. What do we know about these assholes who have Cake?" I asked. "Because they are no longer in the spot where Malice and Cake got ambushed at. I already had that spot checked out and it's empty as fuck."

"Some brother and sister team," Bandz explained. "They've been making silent moves but leaving a trail behind as they go. I don't have much information about them right now. However, I know where their stash house is."

"Well let's get locked and loaded, hitting them bitches in they pockets," Kapri suggested. "I'm sure that'll flush them out."

"I'm sure it will too."

We took two bulletproof jeeps and a shit load of guns with ammunition. We were ready to demolish this place if need be, dressed in all black with body armor looking like the police. Kapri had us hooked up on some boss nicca shit, looking like actual cops. We got out of the vehicles like a tactical unit, making our move like dirty cops. Quickly, the three men sitting out front were sprayed with mace and knocked out with tear gas. Bandz kicked the door in and we made our way inside with our guns drawn.

"Hands up!" Kapri yelled, moving like a real officer. He looked the part which made me wonder if he had formal training.

"Don't shoot," a woman screamed, falling to the floor.

"What do you want?" another woman yelled, with her hands in the air.

"We want the money and the cash," Sir declared. "Give us

what we want and nobody gets hurt."

Tec and Bandz started collecting the money and dope, interrogating them for information, while Kapri and I checked the rest of the place out. Just as we suspected, Cake wasn't there. We rounded up all the people and brought them to the living room and tied them all up. Once we got the information that we needed, we left as fast as we came, retreating back to the warehouse.

"Look at all this money and dope," Sir marveled. "They were doing well for a small-time operation."

"Round that shit up,' Kapri ordered. "Where is Benz's cousin being held?"

I was just about to ask that same thing. I didn't give a fuck about the money or the dope. I just wanted my cousin to be back home with his family, safe and sound, where he belonged.

Sir shrugged and I felt slightly defeated.

"Yo, this shit ain't over. I'm working on the next plan now," Kapri said.

"Listen, bro, we're going to find your cousin," Bandz reassured me.

I nodded, but his words didn't make me feel better. I was going to be a nervous wreck until I saw Cake was alive and away from the niccas who kidnapped him. As Kapri went over the next plan of attack, I dwelled on my guilt. I felt awful that I didn't look for Cake sooner. I can't imagine how he felt. Alone.

Upset. Thinking that I don't care whether he lived or died. I fucked up in a major way.

"It's going to be okay, bruh," Bands reiterated.

For some reason when he said that shit, I felt it. Hearing his genuine concern made a difference. We might not have seen each other in years, but the bond that we had from way back remained strong. That's how shit was. If I rocked with you, I rocked with you. No matter how long I went without seeing you, we always picked up where we left off.

"We're all here for you," Tec confirmed.

Kapri smiled and nodded and Sir patted me on the back.

I felt the love at that moment. These niccas were putting their lives on the line for my cousin. They could have abandoned me and gave up, but they didn't. That shit was real. I'll never forget them because they had my back when I needed them the most.

"I need to take this," Kapri said, walking away with the phone to his ear.

Sir, Tec, Bandz, and I chatted it up until he got back seven minutes later.

"I got the next move," Kapri said. "I'm not sure how much you're going to like this.

He was looking right at me and I knew shit was about to get real different.

"Go ahead. Say what you got to say."

He sighed. "I found your cousin. He's alive, but he's heavily guarded. The only way to get to him is to act as if you're about to do a drug deal with them. They won't suspect anything because they think that crooked cops raided the last spot."

"What about my cover being blown? They know what I look like."

"Not really. We can fix you up so that you won't look like yourself. A heavy beard and a man weave will do the trick."

"Say what now?"

Bandz, Sir, and Tec laughed.

"I don't know why you're laughing," Kapri urged. "You're getting the same thing," he said to Tec.

"Damn. Okay," Tec groveled. "The shit ain't that funny now that I'm in the hot seat too."

"Congratulations, nicca," I joked with Tec.

Kapri ran down the plan as Tec and I dreaded doing this shit.

"I can get you and Tec in, but you two are going to have to do the rest. We'll be on the outside, but one false move, and shit will go left. If I don't see you again, it was a pleasure."

"Fuck that," I let Kapri know. "I'ma come out of this shit alive with Tec and my cousin by my side."

"I like your confidence," Kapri said. "I hope you're right. These are some dangerous people."

"Shit, we're dangerous too," I warned.

# Princess Diamond

The plan sounded dangerous and uneventful, to say the least. However, I was willing to make that sacrifice for my cousin. It was the least I could do. I knew the risks, but I intended on surviving this bullshit with my close friend and cousin escaping as well. It was time for me to live up to my street credibility. Shit was about to get all the way real.

Tec and I walked through the airport to meet up with the so-called buyer. I had a feeling it was the same niccas that took Cake. We walked coolly through O'Hare airport until we got to the dude we were supposed to meet up with. I wasn't sure if it was the guy that we were looking for or not. He invited us to an empty hanger at the airport where we were patted down and searched. I was about to speak when guns were pointed at Tec and me. The suitcases that we had full of money were taken away, and we were nudged toward a car that just pulled up.

"This wasn't the deal," I debated. "I didn't agree to none of this shit."

The heavyset dude to my right pulled out a taser and hit Tec and I with the voltage until we both fell to the ground in shock.

I woke up and saw Tec tied up in one corner and Cake beaten badly and unconscious in another corner. I hadn't been touched, which made me even more suspicious.

"Do you even know why you're alive right now?" the man asked.

"No, but I'm sure you're going to tell me."

"I want you to close down all of your traps and work for me."

"You might as well kill me because that's not going to happen."

"Don't threaten me. I'll do it for real."

"How do I know you won't do it anyway? Ain't that what this is all about?"

I looked around the room at the two heavyset dudes that I recognized from the airport I guess they were his security.

"This is about my mother and father dying in your trap."

"What?" I asked oblivious to what he just said.

"The two crackheads that your cousin Cake killed inside of your trap. The ones he claimed were stealing dope from him."

"So, we're about to go to war over two crackheads?"

"They weren't just any crackheads. They were my mother and father."

I know the look on my face told it all. This shit just kept getting worse and worse. It all made sense now because Cake killed them. Now, I see why they wanted revenge.

"I'm offering your life in exchange for doing business with my sister and me."

"What about my cousin and my friend?"

"They die. I can only spare you."

"No deal," I exclaimed.

The sister appeared out of nowhere. "Enough talking. Kill him and make his friend and his cousin watch."

The two bodyguards grabbed me. Just before the sister was about to shoot me, I moved and she shot one of the bodyguards instead. Tec, who I didn't even know was up, tripped the other big dude and he fell, shaking the floor. His gun fell and I shot at the brother, striking him in the arm. Then, I flipped over and popped the big dude that had just fallen.

Tec grabbed a gun from the floor and shot the brother again while I hit the sister with two bullets to the chest. They both slumped to the floor. Kapri, Sir, and Bandz busted inside of the rundown house, pointing their guns, ready to take more lives.

"Are you, okay?" Kapri asked, dropping his gun to his side.

"Yeah. I'm good. I just hate that my cousin is badly beaten."

"True, but at least he's alive. Don't shoot the messenger, but I thought he was dead."

I glared at Kapri and he didn't seem to have any emotion behind his last statement.

"Cake," I called out.

His eyes were swollen shut and he had marks all over his body. He looked horrible, but at least he was still alive.

"Thanks," he mumbled when I got next to him. "I thought I was going to die."

"Nah. I got here as soon as I could."

He cracked a small smile. I could hardly see it because his lips were swollen like balloons.

# Chapter 13

## Barbie Bennett

"I can't believe Lillian is getting married," Corset said while getting out of my car.

"I know right," I conceded. "She had a horrible streak before her husband to be."

"Facts. That last nicca was a straight loser. Not only did he ghost her, but he also had the nerve to pop up at her house with a sob story every few months asking for money. Ain't no way."

"You got that right, girl. I would have beat the black off his ass. He definitely wouldn't show up at my crib or nobody I know crib ever again."

"Hopefully, this man is the one and she never has to go through that shit ever again."

"I agree."

Corset and I shared a laugh before we checked ourselves out in the mirror and touched up our makeup before going into the church. Lillian's theme was navy, black, and cream.

Certainly, I wouldn't have picked those colors, but to each its own. Lucky for her, she pulled it off, barely. The primary color was navy with cream accents. The bridesmaids and the groomsmen had on navy and cream. Lillian and her husband Ralph were wearing cream. The church and the rest of the decorations and party favors had navy with black accents.

"I thought she was insane when she told me her colors," Corset announced.

"Me too. I'm shocked that she pulled it off. It actually looks nice," I said with surprise.

"Oh there is Rozi and Koda." Corset waved at them. "We should go join them."

"You do that. I'm going to say congratulations to the bride. Then, I'll join you."

"Okay," Corset affirmed, raising her long fitted navy dress so that she could walk over to Rozi and Jakoda.

Originally, my cousins and I were supposed to be a part of the wedding party, but Lillian had a million bridesmaids and not enough groomsmen, so her husband wasn't having it. She had to get rid of us in the bridal party, but we weren't tripping. We still looked better than all of the women up there put together.

I maneuvered through the crowd of people in the corridor and made my way to where Lillian was. It was a side room where she was getting dressed. The moment I walked in, I was in awe. Looking at her took my breath away.

117

"You look so beautiful," I commented.

"Thanks, Barbie. I'm nervous as fuck. I'm so glad to see you."

After she cussed realizing that we were in a church, she covered her mouth and we both laughed.

"You look awesome," I beamed.

Lillian hugged me. "I appreciate that. I feel so bloated and fat. I gave up on my diet weeks ago and said the hell with it. Either I fit in my dress or I don't." She leaned in a little closer whispering for dramatic effect. "Don't tell nobody, but I'm two seconds from busting out of this dress."

We shared another laugh.

"I can't tell. You're holding up well. I just wanted to say congratulations. Everything looks so amazing."

"You don't know how hard this has been. I just wanted the perfect wedding and it's been a journey. My mother, his mother, and all the extra input."

"You pulled it off. How did you do it?"

"Girl, boo. I didn't do this. I hired someone. The perfect wedding planner goes a long way." She looked at my hand and gasped. "That's right, you're engaged. I totally forgot. Congratulations to you. I'll be standing where you are and you'll be in my shoes real soon."

I smiled. "You're right. I'm nervous about it all. I was wondering how Corset and I were going to plan this thing by ourselves."

"Oh girl don't stress yourself. I'll introduce you to my wedding planner. I'm sure she'll be at the reception. She's a godsend. If anyone can get the job done, it's her."

I totally agreed because I never thought her color scheme would look so nice. This woman had to be a miracle worker to pull those colors off.

There was a knock at the door. A woman peeked in. She looked like one of the ushers. "The ceremony is about to start."

"Thank you," Lillian stated, taking a deep breath.

I hugged her. "You'll be fine. See you out there."

I left from the quarters and took my seat next to my cousins. Jakoda spoke to me as soon as I sat down, but Rozi gave me her ass to kiss. She still wasn't speaking to me because of what happened to Sabre. I had apologized a million times. I even offered as much of my time to help out with whatever she was needing like babysitting, grocery shopping, and sitting with Sabre to give Rozi a break since I was on medical leave from work. Rozi still despised me. At this point, I couldn't worry about it. She'd come around eventually.

The ceremony was utterly beautiful. Everything went without a hitch. Now, we were at the reception, partying our asses off. The food was plentiful just like the drinks. People were dancing, singing, turning up, and living in the moment.

"This is so nice," Corset exclaimed, taking a sip of her

champagne. "It makes me wonder if I'll ever find love like Lillian did."

"I'm sure you will."

"I mean, I want something like you and Benz have. I thought I had that with Cake, but you know how he is. The off and on shit with him is too much. I deserve better. Besides, he's still dating that one bitch that I can't stand. I think her name is Shashika or Tashila or some shit. That nicca is confused. He don't know what he wants."

"You will find the perfect man for you. I'm certain of that."

Corset leaned in and gave me a one-armed hug. "That's why you're my favorite cousin."

I winked at her. "Back at cha, cuzo."

"Oh, he's cute. I'll see you later. I just might meet my future husband right now."

I giggled as Corset finished off her drink and walked sexily over to one of the groomsmen. Strolling around the reception hall, I checked out all the array of flowers and the décor, thinking about what I wanted for my wedding and reception. I was standing off by myself, sipping on my champagne lost in my thoughts when someone approached me.

"I hope you're looking around because you like what you see."

I giggled. "That obvious, huh?"

"Yes, but I won't tell nobody if you don't."

"Actually, I was admiring how well put together everything is. Trying to take ideas. I'm engaged," I said bashfully.

"Oh," she said looking down at my ring. "That thing could put someone's eye out."

"True," I giggled. "I have thoughts about hiding it in my purse when I travel sometimes, afraid that someone might try to rob me."

"Are you thinking about hiring a wedding planner?" she asked boldly.

"Why yes I am. Do you have any suggestions?"

I watched as she spun around in her navy fitted dress that clung to her shape like a second skin. "You're looking at her."

"No. You're the one who planned all this?" I assumed.

She took a sip of her champagne and gloated. "I don't like to pat myself on the back, but I do an incredible job."

I was in awe. "Yes you do. It looks expensive, tho."

"I'm sure your husband to be will be glad to splurge. After all, it's your wedding day. Everything has to be perfect."

"Now, you sound like my cousin Corset. That's what she said."

"Your cousin seems like a very smart woman."

"She is, but I don't know about a wedding planner."

"What's there to think about?"

I shrugged. My gut said not to do it. I wasn't sure why, but my heart had already fell in love with what I saw. I wanted the same thing.

I guess she must've sensed my hesitation. Reaching into her clutch, she pulled out her business card. "Why don't you take my card?"

"Designs by Che," I said aloud.

"Yes. Everyone calls me Che, but my real name is Dache. I hate my real name. If you ever call me that, I might have to kill you."

She laughed and I laughed too, but chills went down my spine as she spoke. Something about her tone said she wasn't joking even though she was laughing and smiling.

"Fine by me. Your secret is safe with me, Che," I reassured. "I won't tell a soul."

"I understand you might be hesitant about my prices, but I can produce weddings at any budget. I know how to turn fifteen cents into a dollar. That's why I'm the best at what I do. If you want an affordable dream wedding, I can make that happen as well."

"Now, you're talking my language."

"Good. Why don't you give me a call? If you're busy, I can come to you if you like and bring my work with me. I'm very flexible."

I stared at her card which was beautifully designed as well. "Sure. I'd like that. I'll call you to set something up."

"Sounds like a plan. Oh, I'm Barbie by the way. I forgot to

introduce myself."

She grinned as if she already knew who I was. "Nice to finally meet you, Barbie."

"Girl, where have you been?" Corset asked, fanning herself. "We're about to do the Electric Slide."

I turned my head to introduce Che to Corset, but she was gone, like she had disappeared into thin air. I thought nothing of it as Corset drug me towards the dance floor so we could show these old timers how to get down.

### *•.¸♡ Barbie & Benz ♡¸.•*

Benz and I were laying in my bed at my place. He said he had to get his carpet cleaned. I didn't know what that was all about. However, I was happy that he was with me and we were cuddling and not having sex. I know this whole abstinence thing was hard on him. I didn't want to push the envelope. Things were going great with us. He hadn't asked for sex and I wasn't about to give it.

Benz picked up two glasses of champagne and handed me a glass. "Toast to the most beautiful woman in the world."

"Toast to the most loving man in the world."

We clinked our glasses and took a sip.

Benz picked up one of the chocolate-covered strawberries and fed it to me. "My beautiful queen tell me all about your day."

I grabbed my chest and swiveled my neck after taking a bite of the strawberry. "Who is this man and what have you done with Benz?"

He chuckled and took a bite of the same chocolate covered strawberry that he fed me. "I just wanted to show you that I heard you. I'm in this for the long haul. If you say no sex, then it's no sex until we're married. I love you. I will do what it takes not only to prove that to you, but I want to be the best husband that I can be. Discipline is the key sometimes and I know that being a dog in the past got me into a lot of trouble. I don't want to be that man anymore. I want to be a faithful, loving husband, but that doesn't mean that I can't spoil my woman and marinate that pussy until we do connect physically."

I giggled, falling back on the bed. "You're so full of shit. You talked to my father, didn't you?"

Benz exhaled dramatically and looked at me with a crazy ass face. "So, what if I did."

I fell out laughing again. Between his response, the look on his face, and what I already knew, I couldn't contain myself.

"Oh, so you think this shit is fun and giggles. Fuck you, Barbie. Get on my fuckin' nerves."

Benz was upset and I was still laughing. I had to get out all of my laughter before I addressed him. Scooting next to him. I put my arm around his neck and stared into his eyes.

"I think what you're doing is great, babe."

"Nah, nicca, your ass was laughing and whatnot. This muthafuckin' shit is hard. You acting like we're exercising or some shit. My dick be hard all the fuckin' time and I gotta talk him off the ledge."

I straighten up my face because I knew this was hard for Benz. "I'm sorry for laughing, babe. I know how hard this is for you. I love you even more for doing it."

Benz perched his lips even more, letting me know that I had to do more ass kissing.

"And I promise to be everything and more on our honeymoon. Super wet and juicy, just the way you like it."

"I can cum in your mouth?" Benz asked eagerly as if that was his dying wish.

"Yes, baby. You can cum in my mouth, all over my face or whatever else you want to. I'll be Mrs. Sorensen then, so shit gone get nasty between us. Our honeymoon night will be dedicated to you."

Benz grinned. "That's what I'm talking about. I'ma start planning that shit now. I can't wait. It's gone be lit."

I was glad he was in a better mood because I wanted to talk to him about wedding stuff. I knew how men could be when women mentioned dresses and cake tasting. They aren't interested at all in the planning. I wanted Benz to be a part of the process despite what I know.

"I met a wedding planner at Lillian's wedding today. How do you feel about that?"

"I don't. That's you and your cousin's shit. Y'all plan it and I will show up. End of the discussion."

"Um, it's not like that. This is your wedding too. What you want matters too."

"Babe, I want whatever you want. At the end of the day, I just want to put a ring on your finger and give you my last name."

"It's that simple?"

"For me it is."

"I hear you, but I want you involved. I'm setting up a meeting with the wedding planner, and you're paying for it."

"I'll pay for whatever you want. However, I'm not sure if I can be there for you the way you want me to. I have a lot going on in the streets. That shit needs to be taken care of before we get married."

"I understand, but you'll try though."

"Of course."

# Chapter 14

## Brysen "Benz" Sorensen

Shit was still fucked up in the streets, but I wasn't going to let that stop me from supporting my little brother. After the doctor told Malice that there was a strong possibility that he might not walk again, he was more determined than ever to prove the doctor wrong. When he looked me in my eyes and told me that he was going to walk again, I knew I had to support him. I got him admitted to the best rehabilitation program in the city. If my brother was that determined to get back on his feet, literally, then I needed to do everything humanly possible to make his dream a reality.

Malice was doing a combination of traditional therapy and aquatic therapy to maximize his recovery. It consisted of daily therapy walks with his crutches, alternate kicking motions, and approved treadmill exercises. Most days, Malice was exhausted because the therapy pushed his endurance to the limit.

I came as often as I could to his rehab visits. He had a room here at the facility so often he stayed overnight if the therapy got to be too much, and he felt too weak to go home. Other times, he completed his sessions at home with his wife and kids. He didn't want to be totally confined to a facility because the baby's due date was quickly approaching. Behati only had two more weeks. I accompanied them to the last doctor's appointment. Everything was going well. Behati and the baby were both doing great.

Today, Malice was in the pool with two therapists. He said he liked the water therapy the most because his muscles were more relaxed, and he felt that he could move better inside the pool. I noticed a difference when he started increasing his aquatic therapy. He seemed more balanced and stronger than when he did his traditional therapy.

"Yo, bro, you might be running the next time I come visit."

Malice laughed. "I just might be. You know how I am. I move in silence anyway."

I chuckled. I was so happy to see my brother in great spirits. He handled this whole situation so well. Had it been me, I would have been angry at the world.

"Can't nobody hold me down," Malice chuckled.

"Damn right."

I waited patiently in Malice's room while the therapists helped him out of the pool, dried him off, and helped him dress. Afterwards, he was placed into his motorized wheelchair. He zoomed back to his room and I followed him.

"Are you ready for me to take you home?"

"Nah, not yet," he yawned. "I need to get a nap in. That water ain't no joke."

"Aight. Just call me when you're ready."

Malice yawned again and I could tell that he wasn't going to be awake too much longer. "Can you do me a favor, bro?"

"Of course. Anything."

"Can you take Behati to her doctor's appointment? I was supposed to go with her, but I couldn't reschedule my therapy. It's like every nicca in here wants to be in the pool because they witness my progress."

I laughed. "You can't be hating on people if they want to achieve the same success. That's petty, bro."

"Whatever. I just know that nobody wanted to do the shit when I got here, now the shit is filled up to the max. I can barely get my sessions in."

"As much as these muthafuckas getting paid, they better squeeze you in. Don't make me hack into their system to erase some shit."

Malice shook his head. "And who is petty now?"

We both laughed.

"You didn't even have to ask about Behati, bro. If she needs me, you know I'm there."

Malice's eyes were closing. "Thanks, bro. You're the best."

I kissed my brother on his forehead as he drifted off to

sleep. I used to think that shit was gay until I almost lost him. Now, I don't give a fuck who thinks what. I'ma show my little brother as much love as possible.

I called Behati on my way over to pick her up. "Malice is taking a nap at the facility. I'm not sure if he'll be strong enough to make it back home tonight or not. He was in the water today."

"I kinda figured that," she answered, sounding completely out of breath."

"Why do you sound like that?"

"Like what?" she questioned.

"Like you've been running a mile."

She giggled. "Oh, it's nothing. The life of a mom of three with one more on the way." She giggled again. "This is everyday stuff for me."

I didn't want to sound alarming, but I was concerned. "I've talked to you plenty of times while you were keeping up with the kids and you never sounded this winded. Do you feel okay?"

"Yes. I feel fine. I'm surprised that I sound winded."

I heard the doorbell ring.

"That's your dad. I gotta go. He's going to look after the kids while I go to my doctor's appointment."

"Actually, that's why I called. I'm on my way to pick you up. I'm taking you."

"Benz, I can go by myself. I'm a big girl. I had three other kids. You and Malice are treating me as if I'm handicapped. I feel absolutely fine."

"Well, you don't sound fine."

"I was just at the doctor three days ago. She said the baby and I are doing great. I'm sure Malice told you that. You're getting all worked up over nothing."

"Maybe so, but I'm taking you anyway. Don't argue with me. I'll see you in a minute."

Behati sighed and hung up. This baby had her getting beside herself. She had lost her mind hanging up on me. I wasn't Malice, I'd get in her ass. Unfortunately, I was more concerned with her health right now, so chewing her out over something petty would have to wait.

When my father opened the door, I saw why Behati was out of breath. Mally was crawling around everywhere, scooting and rolling like a puppy. The girls were playing with streamers and doing flips everywhere. My dad looked as if he was going to pull his hair out and Behati was reprimanding the kids to pick shit up. Basically, Malice's crib was a fucking mad house. It was times like this that I regretted having his back because there is no way I wanted to be here at his house. He needed to get well soon so he could deal with his moody ass wife and bad ass kids.

"I'm ready," Behati said, putting on her coat.

Even as she spoke then, she seemed as if she wasn't fully catching her breath. I didn't mention it again, I was going to pull the doctor aside and tell her what I heard. It might not be nothing, but then again, I wasn't about to take those chances.

I kissed my bad ass nephew and nieces and gave my pops a hug before I accompanied Behati to my vehicle. I offered to carry her purse that looked like a suitcase, but she insisted on keeping it on her shoulder.

As we drove, I noticed that Behati's breathing was getting more noticeable. I kept glancing at her as she played with her phone. She seemed oblivious to it all. The shit was so apparent that it had me nervous. I didn't know whether to take her to the emergency room or to the doctor's office. I kept on thinking what would Malice do. At this point, I had no clue because he was a husband and I wasn't. I knew what he'd do when it came to street shit, but this marriage shit was for the birds. The whole situation had me second guessing my proposal because Barbie was twice as moody as Behati.

I kept my mouth shut as we rode to her doctor's appointment, I even kept my mouth shut when we went inside for her check-up. She glanced at me as if I was going to stay in the waiting room, and I gave her a look that said don't test me if you know what's good. She lowered her eyes and walked to the assigned patient room without saying another word. I was coming back here with her whether she liked it or not. I was representing Malice because he couldn't be here.

Behati was talking to the doctor when her energy shifted. She was about to get off the table when the doctor noticed what I had been indicating all along.

"When did the shortness of breath start?" she asked.

Behati was about to play the same game with me, but the doctor wasn't having it, giving her that look.

Behati sighed in defeat. "Earlier this morning."

I glared at her because I felt something was wrong all along.

"It's probably nothing but let me take your vitals to be sure."

"Is everything okay, doc?" I asked, feeling very concerned.

The doctor's face told it all. "Um, I'm not sure." She tried to remain calm, but I felt the panic in the room. "Can you make sure she gets to the hospital? I'll be there shortly to check on her. I'm calling in a few tests for her, just to be sure."

Behati was now alarmed. "Is something wrong?"

The blood looked as if it had drained from the doctor's face, but she was still speaking in a calm voice. "Um, don't worry, it's just a few tests. I want to make sure you and the baby are okay. I want you to wear this oxygen mask just in case."

I helped Behati off the table, and I knew something wasn't right. Before I could ask her how she was feeling, she collapsed in my arms.

"I'm calling an ambulance," her doctor said.

"It's no time for that. The hospital is right down the street," I urged. "Why don't I drive, and you hop in the back with her.

You said you were going to meet us there anyway."

"That's true. Let's do it."

I carried Behati to my car, nervous as all outdoors as her doctor followed right behind me. I put my sister-in-law in the back seat and hopped in. Her doctor got in as well, tending to her in the back. She called in the emergency while I drove like a bat out of hell. I'm sure this white woman was scared out of her mind by the time I pulled up to the emergency room doors. Staff was already there waiting for us. Thank goodness her doctor had accompanied her because I didn't have a clue what to do. Driving her here in a rush was easy, but telling the staff what was going on, that was another story all together.

Behati's doctor instructed the medical staff that her oxygen levels were low. She started calling out all the tests that she wanted ran when Behati passed out. Now, I was freaking out. They had to intubate her, and I was completely freaking out.

"She's unresponsive," her doctor announced.

They were moving so fast that I didn't have time to let anyone know what was going on. I just held onto her suitcase looking purse and traveled behind everyone as they rushed down the hospital hallways. I was shoved back when I reached a point that only medical staff could were allowed.

"There is a waiting room to your left. Have a seat. We'll update you as soon as we can," a nurse stated.

The hospital doors closed, and I felt helpless. Immediately,

I called my dad and told him what was going on. I would have called Behati's parents, but they were in Africa. Wasn't no sense of worrying them right now. Next, I called Barbie and filled her in. She said she was on her way. Finally, I took a deep breath and called Malice. The rehabilitation facility said he was still sleep, but they would take a message. I figured he was so I told them not to wake him and to have him call me back when he woke up.

I sat there waiting for hours on an update. By now, Barbie had joined me and my father with the kids. We were all sitting in the waiting area together again. Mally was sleep, thank goodness. My nieces were on their tablets playing e-learning games, so they were quiet. My father, Barbie, and I seemed lost in our own thoughts, not saying a word. Finally, her doctor entered to give us an update.

"She had a clot that traveled to her lungs. We've fished it out, but..."

"How's the baby?" Barbie, my father, and I asked at the same time.

Dr. Herman lowered her gaze before speaking to us again. "Is the husband here yet?"

"No," I replied. "Not yet."

"Well, in his absence only one of you can come back. Who wants to come?"

"I'll do it," I offered. I didn't want to be stuck with my

nieces and nephew, cramped up in this small space. I needed to get the hell out of here. They were about to turn up any minute now.

"I'll do it," my father said. "I'm the most experienced one here."

I flopped down about to call Malice again when he came zooming in on his motorized wheelchair. "I'm here, Dr. Herman. How are my wife and son?"

The worried look on Dr. Herman's face told it all before she even opened her mouth. "We had to perform an emergency C-Section on your wife. She'll be on blood thinners and bedrest for about a week. We're going to monitor her for the next forty-eight hours, and if everything checks out, she'll be able to leave."

"That sounds like good news for my wife. What about my son?" Malice asked once again.

"There were some complications."

We all gasped anticipating the doctor's next word.

"Your son is in NICU. He wasn't getting enough oxygen."

"Can I see him?"

"Unfortunately, you can see your wife, but not the baby."

"Can we all go?" I asked. "We all want to see her too."

Dr. Herman must've noticed the desperation on our faces and waved us to follow her. Malice led the way, zooming ahead. We walked into the room where Behati was and saw her hooked up to a few machines. She was wearing oxygen as well. Malice zoomed over to her side, holding her hand and reassuring her that everything is going to be alright.

The energy in the room was fucked up. Everyone was on the brink of tears. My father did the only thing we could do in a moment like this which was to pray. He asked us all to gather, hold hands, and bow our heads while he said the most heartfelt prayer. As he prayed, I felt the spirit of God in the room. Silently, I thanked the Lord. I'm sure if I felt His presence, Malice and Behati felt His presence too.

Shortly after we prayed, Dr. Herman came into the room with the baby in her arms. "This little guy is a fighter. Not only did his vitals miraculously improve, but he is also breathing on his own too. Looks like he made a full recovery in a matter of minutes."

Dr. Herman handed the baby boy to Behati and she lowered the baby so that Malice could see his son.

"What are you going to name him?" Dr. Herman asked.

Malice stared at the baby and then at me. "There is only one person that I know who has that type of fight. This person always beats the odds. The baby's name is Benzo. Named appropriately after his uncle who has the same will and fight to survive no matter what."

Behati handed the baby to me, and I almost broke the fuck down. Baby Benzo rested comfortably in my arms as I silently continued to thank God for the safety of my sister-in-law and my namesake. My little nephew had a nicca feeling sappy like a damn Hallmark movie and shit.

# Chapter 15

## Barbie Bennett

I had just finished baking cookies and brewing coffee when the doorbell rang. I was sure it was Che, and I was so excited. I smoothed down my skirt and glanced at myself in my hallway mirror before opening the door.

"Hey," I said with a welcoming smile.

"Hi," she replied with a mutual grin. "I hope I'm not too early."

"No. You're right on time. Come in."

"Wow," she beamed, straining her neck to look around. "This place is fabulous. I saw when they were building these condos, but I had no idea it would be this luxurious inside."

My smile widened. "Thank you. They are quite nice. I had first dips on this place because I'm in real estate."

"Oh, really."

I nodded. "Yes. I sold one of the properties around the corner to a client and when this one became available, I decided to snatch it up for myself."

"Well good for you. A lady that knows what she wants. That's awesome."

Che followed me into the living room where I offered her a seat.

"I'll be right back."

I went to the kitchen to get the cookies and the coffee, but it was still brewing so I brought the plate of cookies and two bottle waters, sitting it all down before her.

"I hope you like cookies. I have chocolate chip and oatmeal raisin."

"Yes, I do. Thank you. Did you make them from scratch?"

"Yes, My grandmother's recipe."

Che picked up one of the cookies taking a bite. "Mmmm. Delicious."

"Thank you."

"Is your fiancé going to join us?"

"No. He has business to take care of."

"Oh really, what kind of business is he into."

"Online gaming primarily. He has other ventures that he goes into with friends to make money. I don't ask and he doesn't tell."

Che looked at me oddly and smiled. "So, tell me about you and the hubby-to-be. I want to get a clear idea of who you two are, so I can envision what the wedding will be like."

"Sure. Um, Benz and I have known each other since we were younger. We started out as friends, but I was the first one to realize that I felt something more for him. I didn't act on it right away because he didn't seem interested. Finally, I got up the courage to confess my love. Things weren't as smooth as they are now, but finally he popped the question and now I'm planning a wedding."

"What about kids? Do either of you have kids?"

I cleared my throat, trying not to cry. "I was pregnant, but I had a miscarriage."

Che stopped eating her cookie. "I'm so sorry to hear that."

I wiped away a tear about to fall and smiled despite my pain. "Everything happens for a reason. I understand that now. At the time, I was so hurt, but God has a plan. As much as I wanted our baby, I'm sure that I will be blessed even more because of it.

"Hmmm. And how does Benz feel about that? Is he upset with you that you lost the baby? Or is he ready to make another one right away?"

"No. Benz is very supportive. In fact, he has agreed to wait until marriage to have sex again."

"Hmmm. Was that your idea or his?"

"It was mine," I replied, a little taken aback by all the questions. "Where is this conversation going? I'm starting to feel uncomfortable."

Che looked up at me and grinned. "I assure you that was not my intention. I was simply trying to get to know you both."

I was looking at her with inquisitive eyes demanding her to go into detail.

"Let me explain. Every couple has a story and that story helps me communicate the love that they have for each other at the wedding. I work based on vibes and energy. Basically, I'm just trying to feel you two out as a couple so that I can show off the artistic design for the world as you share nuptials. I hope you don't mind my process. I didn't mean to offend you."

I calmed down a little. I was ready to beat this bitch's face in until she explained. What she said made sense. Getting married was a whole vibe, and I wanted our guests to experience our wedding day organically. Even though, everyone that would be invited shared a special connection with us. They deserved to be there and witness our special moment.

"Point well taken," I commented.

"Listen, I don't mean any harm. I just want to give you the day of your dreams. Sometimes my methods are a little unconventional, but I mean well. At the end of the day, I work for you and whatever you say goes. I too feel your energy and produce that to the world on your special day."

I wasn't even mad anymore. What she said was resonating with me. I think she truly had a gift because instead of wanting to throw her out, I wanted to hear more about her ideas regarding my wedding. She didn't know it yet, but she definitely convinced me.

"Let's make this official. You're hired," I beamed.

"No," Che said, taken aback.

"Honestly, I thought you were going to ask me to leave. I was playing it cool, but deep down inside I was nervous that I had lost you as a client."

"No. I totally get where you're coming from. You seem to care about your work. That would explain why you ask so many questions. At the end of the day, I can tell that you and I have the same goal, planning my perfect wedding day."

"Most definitely. I'm seeing so many things after you opening up and told me your story. Thank you for being so understanding."

I felt like a fool for jumping to conclusions. The bad vibe that I had in the pit of my stomach was all for nothing. Che just meant well. Was she a little out of the norm for the way she did things? Certainly. Yet and still, I wasn't one to judge because I didn't like people who assumed or judged me. As long as Che made my wedding look as fabulous as Lillian's, I was okay with her peculiar methods.

My phone rang. It was Benz.

"Excuse me. I need to take this."

I rushed to the kitchen to answer the phone.

"Where are you? Che has been here."

"I'm not going to make it. Something came up."

"Something more important than our wedding. No, but at the same time, it is important. I hope you understand. I'm sure you're doing a great job without me. I'll try to make it next time."

"You're a bad liar. I know you didn't want to meet with her. I'll bet in your mind you consider this woman stuff."

"Baby, listen, I never said that. You did. I just called to tell you that I won't make it in time to speak with the wedding planner."

I sighed, but I already had a feeling that he wasn't coming. "Whatever. You better bring me home a steak dinner."

"As you wish, one expensive steak dinner coming up."

I giggled. Benz was such a character. "Whatever. Don't be out too late."

"Yes, my lady. I promise to come home at a decent hour with your steak dinner in hand."

His English accent made me giggle even more. "You are so stupid. I'll talk to you later. I'm still with Che."

"Okay, baby, I love you."

"I love you too. Now go plan our extraordinary wedding."

I hung up the phone and went back into the room where Che was. She was blowing her nose and wiping away tears. I wasn't sure what had happened because I hadn't been gone that long.

"Did I miss something?" I asked her with caution.

"No. I got a call while you were gone. My cousin just passed. He was shot and killed during my time here."

I gasped. I could only imagine how I would feel if my cousin was shot and killed while I was out somewhere. "If you need to leave, I can reschedule for another time."

"Thanks. That's so nice of you. I appreciate it. I'm not myself anymore. All I can think about is my cousin."

"No biggie. Go on and go. I'll call you tomorrow with a follow up appointment."

"I appreciate that." Che stood to her feet, gathering her stuff. "Talk to you next time."

"Okay, bye."

I walked her to the door and watched her walk to her vehicle. I felt some type of way about our meeting, but I didn't know why. Was it her unconventional methods that rubbed me the wrong way? I sighed and tried to shake the bad feeling. Maybe I was just having wedding day jitters. In fact, that would make sense. I had been thinking about the big day all week long. The fact that I wanted things to be perfect could be getting to me.

# Chapter 16

## Brysen "Benz" Sorensen

Rozi had to be out of her mind if she thought my boy, the guy I considered family was going to be laid up in the hospital shot, and I didn't come to visit. I guess she forgot I knew Sabre before he was her husband. She, nor her pettiness was going to stop me from spending time with my homie.

Sabre got out of the hospital a couple days ago, but I couldn't come by until Rozi was gone. She still hated me and Barbie. We had to sneak around Rozi's stank attitude and the times she came to visit, so we didn't run into her. Thank goodness for Corset. She ran interference for Barbie and me so that we could visit Sabre. We weren't able to stay long, but at least my boy knew that we didn't abandon him in his time of need.

I parked my car down the street and got out looking around for Rozi like the Feds was on my ass. In fact, I think she was worse than the Feds. Her stubbornness and longevity to hold a grudge exceeded a Fed case by all means.

"Hey, bro," Sabre said, answering the door hunched over in his robe. He had one hand holding the door and the other hand keeping his robe closed.

"Nicca, I can wait a minute if you want to fasten your robe."

"Nah. I'm good, bro. Come on in."

"Listen," I said, looking at his hand that was keeping his robe barely closed. "I'll leave if it's not a good time."

"Nonsense," Sabre exclaimed, waving me in. "It's as good a time as any."

I stepped inside and turned around quickly closing the door. "I'm turning around so that you can get your robe situation together. I didn't come over here to see dick and balls."

Sabre laughed. I assumed he was tying up his robe while I faced the door.

"I'm good, bro. You can turn around now."

I peeked over my shoulder to make sure his robe was tied before I turned around completely.

"How are you, Sab?"

He grinned. "For real, bro, I'm feeling great. I'm blessed to be alive. I feel like God gave me a new lease on life. The air smells different. The world looks different. I even hear shit different."

I chuckled, but I caught myself when Sabre stared at me.

"Bro, I'm not trying to sound insensitive, but you have to admit that what you said sounds a little crazy." I twisted my face as I stared at him.

"I'm being real, bro. You need to respect that."

I nodded. "My bad. I didn't know you were serious. I'll keep the humor to myself. How's recovery?" I asked, changing the subject. I didn't want to upset him in any kind of way.

"Surprisingly, I'm feeling quite well. Tired mostly. Overall blessed."

"Listen, I want to apologize for getting you mixed up into this shit. I had no idea that something so horrific would happen to you."

Sabre waved his hand at me. "I don't blame you. It was an accident."

"I know it was, but still, I feel bad. I'm the one who called you out of retirement to help me. Rozi has a point. I'm responsible for this mess. If it wasn't for me, you wouldn't have gotten shot."

Sabre turned up his lip. "Nah. You didn't force my arm. Yes. You asked me to help you."

I was about to protest when Sabre held up his hand, cutting me off.

"However, I could have said no. You didn't force me. I'm my own man. Truth is, I kind of missed the action. Being a stay-at-home dad isn't easy. I'm a street nicca. That shit flows through my blood. It's all I have ever known. Niccas from where I'm from didn't retire from the game. They either died out the shit or got locked up for the shit."

"Facts, but that makes you a rare breed. You know I don't care much for your wife. She is…"

"Watch it," Sabre reprimanded.

"I was going to say that she might be a pain, but she's right. I couldn't live with myself if something happened to you when you should have been at home tending to your family."

Sabre went to speak, but it was my time to cut him off. "I gotta go. Once we find all these niccas that came at us, you're out the game for good. I don't need you that much. I'd rather have you alive and be at home than to have you dead on my team."

Sabre nodded. "Fair enough."

"Then, it's settled. I'll holler at you later. I got another stop to make."

Sabre walked me to the door. We dapped it up and hugged before I left. I wasn't lying. I had another stop to make since I was on the apology tour. I had to make things right with this person. He meant the world to me and it was time that I expressed that to him.

I drove listening to 2Pac. I had a lot of shit on my mind, and I felt like he was the only one who understood me. This man was a deep prolific poet that put rhyme to music. I identified with him because I felt like he was passionate and invested but misunderstood just like me. At times, I felt like I couldn't trust no one but myself. Then, at the same time, I felt like I was closest to those who loved me the most. I'll admit that I'm a complicated human being that is emotionally charged at times. However, I go hard for those that I love, and I will kill for them even if that means serving jail time.

"What up, bro?" I asked as soon as Cake opened the door.

He didn't look as bad as the day that he was rescued. Still, he had a long way to go to look normal. His face was battered and bruised. One of his eyes was still swollen shut. It wasn't as purple so that was a positive. Then again, he was lucky to be alive and I was thankful for that.


"Yo, what brings you to this neighborhood?" Cake asked, inviting me in.

"I came to see you."

"You lying?"

"Nah, cuzo. I'm not. You were on my mind and I needed to stop by. I hope it's cool."

"Of course."

Cake slowly walked into the living room, and gently sat down on the couch. I could tell that he was still in pain.

"Can I get you anything?"

"Bro, I'm good. If I need something, I'll get it. You just

rest up because I'm going to need you in the future."

Cake nodded.

"Have you seen a doctor yet?"

"Yeah. I had the one on payroll come through a few times. He said nothing is broke. I just look bad and in a lot of pain."

"How much pain?" I asked concerned.

Cake shrugged. "Nothing I can't handle. What's up with you? The streets good? How's Malice?"

I saw right through Cake. He was avoiding the subject. He didn't want to talk about himself, so he deflected.

"Listen, the streets are what they are and Malice is good. I'm sure you already knew that. The reason why I'm here is because I needed to talk to you."

"Yeah. What's up?"

"I wanted to apologize."

"For what?" Cake asked, rubbing his neck.

"For pulling a gun out on you. For not listening to you. For not treating you like a brother. For not looking for you sooner. Do you forgive me?"

Cake looked at me, and I never saw my cousin look so sad. I could tell that I hit an emotional nerve. His eyes fell to the floor and I felt his pain.

"After my brother died, I looked at you and Malice as more than cousins. You two became my brothers. I wanted to belong and be with you all to escape the hole in my heart that Kony left behind. I might not show it the way I should, but I miss him so much. I just wanted you two to fill that void."

I stared at my cousin and for the first time my heart broke. I never felt so much compassion for Cake. I guess I just thought he was so strong that he didn't need the support. He never acted like he did. I guess I was wrong.

"Listen, bro, I'm sorry for everything. When I found out you were really missing, it broke my heart. I felt stupid because I could have been looking for you instead of judging you. I was wrong, and I just need your forgiveness."

Cake got up and slowly walked toward me. For a hot minute, I thought he was going to hit my ass. I would have taken that punch if he did.

"I'm sorry too," he said, sitting on the arm of the chair. "I know I'm not the easiest person to get along with."

"Me either."

"I'm stubborn."

"Me too."

"I'm about this life."

"Me too."

"And I hate taking losses."

"Me too."

Cake stared at me long and hard. "Then, I guess you hate being hurt."

"I do," I agreed.

"I'm only going to admit this once. You hurt me, bro. All I wanted to do was belong with my cousins who I considered my brothers."

I felt bad when he said that. "I should have known better. I wasn't thinking about nobody but myself."

Cake slid down on the loveseat, sitting next to me. I examined his bruised face and weak movements. "I accept your apology. I'll admit, I could have handled everything better too. I think Malice was right."

"What did he say?" I inquired.

"He said we couldn't get along because we were too much alike."

I smirked. "He might have a point."

After the apologies were out of the way, we got in a few games of *NBA 2k* and *Call of Duty*. After two orders of Uber eats, a case of beer, and another trip down memory lane, I was ready to leave Cake's spot. Besides, he was tired. He just didn't want to let me know. I noticed how he kept yawning after he took his pain pill.

"I'ma head out, cuzo. I hope you feel better. I'll check on you later, and don't hesitate to call if you need anything. I mean it."

We slapped hands and one-arm hugged.

"Thanks, bro. That means a lot to me.'

"Good," I exclaimed. "From now on things are going to be

different between us."

"I look forward to it," Cake said, walking me to the door.

I walked onto the porch and heard the door close behind me. The time I spent with Cake felt good. It was something that was long overdue. Feeling like I was on top of the world, I practically skipped to my car. Everything was all sunshine and roses until I saw the note left on my ride. I didn't think nothing of it when I snatched it off my windshield and jumped into my car. I didn't get alarmed until I read the handwritten note. *It said I'm not dead.*

I nearly broke my neck looking around in every direction to see who left this shit. Several things came to my mind. This person followed me over here, and that meant that if my moves were being watched, Barbie was in danger. As soon as I got home, I was going to give Barbie my newest gun. I was going to insist that she kept one on her at all times.

# Chapter 17

## Barbie Bennett

"You better come and get me before I kill this nicca," Corset hollered into the phone.

"Huh? Where you at?"

"Moon's house. He on that extra shit again and I'm about to bust his head wide open."

"Oh, lawd. Don't do nothing too crazy. I'm on my way."

I was barely awake. I had just rolled out of bed, about to take a morning piss when Corset's picture flashed across my screen. I knew it was going to be some dumb shit because she never called me this early in the morning. She always slept in until noon.

I had no idea why she was still messing around with Moon's dog ass. He was way worse than Cake. At least with Cake she knew what she was getting into. With Moon, he was a fat, lying, cheating bastard. I never understood what she saw in this loser ass nicca. All them sugar daddies that she fucked with and she had to fall hard for this piece of shit. He looked like Tracy Morgan in the face, he was built like Faizon Love, and he had a wandering lazy eye like Forest Whitaker. He had a lot of nerve cheating on my cousin. She was too damn pretty to be going through issues with that dusty ass nicca.

I thought about taking my ass back to bed and saying forget Corset and Moon's silly ass shit. Then, I thought about it. Corset might really kill that nicca. Then, I would feel bad because she asked me to come and get her. If she was calling me, that meant he picked her up and she didn't have any money to catch an uber.

After tending to my hygiene, I dressed in some stretchy jeans with rhinestones, a floral tank, and Nike slides. I just got my toes done and I wanted to show them off. I grabbed my bat because if this big nicca got too out of hand, I wasn't going to fight his ass. He was going to catch a beat down.

I heard Corset's loudmouth from the curb. She was cussing Moon out.

"I'm tired of getting the run around Moon. Who is the bitch?"

"We done been through this already. I don't know who you're talking about?"

"Nicca just tell me who the bitch is?"

"Ain't no other bitch. You're the only one for me."

"That's a boldface lie, and you know it. I can smell the

bitch's perfume all up in this muthafucka."

"That's not perfume you're smelling. It's Febreze."

"So, now you think I'ma damn fool."

"I didn't say that, Set. You're putting words into my mouth."

"You didn't have to. You think that I can't smell the difference between air freshener and cheap ass perfume?"

"It's Febreze, for real. A new scent."

"You're just begging for me to fuck you up. The more you lie the angrier I get. I don't understand why you just don't tell the truth."

"I am telling the truth."

I was standing in the doorway contemplating what to do next. They were so into their argument that they didn't even notice that the door was open, and I had already let myself in.

Finally, Corset looked my way. "Hey Barbie. Tell me what it smells like in here to you."

I took a strong whiff. "Some dollar store perfume."

I could have lied and said it smelled like something else, just to keep the peace, but I was going to ride with my cousin no matter what. Since she was with the shits, I was too.

"See, nicca, I told your black ass. That ain't no fuckin' Febreze. You're full of shit."

"Wait. Corset. Calm down. Don't do nothing stupid."

"Too late for that nicca. You should have thought about

that before you brought that bitch to your house."

"Listen, Set, don't show out because Barbie is here now."

Corset looked from him to me and back to him. "Show out. Nicca, I'ma show your ass what the fuck showing out looks like."

"Aw shit," I voiced. "You done fucked up now."

Corset stomped over towards me and took the bat that I was holding onto out of my hand, and started smashing up all of his shit.

"Bitch, you're crazy. Why are you smashing all of my shit?" Moon hollered.

Corset was putting in work. She had broke several vases, two glass end tables, and now she was knocking all of his paintings off the wall. I don't know how Moon managed to the bat away from her, but he did. That was a big mistake because she started hitting him. I mean, she was pushing and slapping him so hard I had to cringe,

"I'm so sick of your lying ass," Corset screamed

"Bitch don't hit me again."

Corset cracked her knuckles and punched Moon right in the head. I didn't mean to laugh, but it was funny. She was jumping around, tagging his ass like a kangaroo.

"Corset," I said calmly. "Let's go before the neighbors call the police. I'm not trying to go to jail."

Moon dropped the bat a long time ago. I picked it up so that

Corset didn't grab it again.

"I'm ready to go, Barbie. This nicca ain't worth my time."

"You bet not leave. Who is going to clean all this shit up?"

"I don't fuckin' know," Corset spat. "Ask that same hoe with the cheap perfume to clean this shit up. And while you're at it ask that hoe to fix those lumps on your head too."

I ushered Corset out of Moon's home. She was still fuming when she got into the car.

"I hate that sorry ass nicca."

"No, you don't. You care about him."

"Fuck him. Niccas ain't shit."

"Girl, why were you over there at Moon's crib anyway."

Corset sucked her teeth. "I had to get away from my mother. She's on my back again about getting a job."

I wanted to bite my tongue, but I couldn't. "Don't you think it's about time? You can't live off your good looks and sugar daddies forever."

Corset cut her eyes at me. "C'mon, Barbie, not you too."

"I'm not trying to jump down your throat like auntie does. I'm just saying that it's time cuzo. You need to have your own money, so you can make your own moves."

Corset exhaled loudly. "I guess you're right. I didn't want to say nothing, but I've been looking into this pharmacy tech program. It's only a few months and I can have a job right away."

"That's what's up." I reached over and hugged her at the light. "Why don't you stay with me tonight?"

"Is it cool? I know you and Benz are trying to rekindle and stuff. I don't want to interfere."

"Girl, boo. He lives right next door. If we want privacy, we can always go to his house. You're more than welcome to come and stay anytime just to get away from auntie."

"Thanks cuzo. I really need the break."

As I drove to my condo, I listened to Corset's plans for the future. She admitted that she was sick of the sugar daddy thing and once she got done with the pharmacy tech program, she was going to be done with that life for good. She talked about cutting off all these niccas and just focusing on herself. She even mentioned moving out of her parent's home and finding her own spot. I was proud of her. She had always been so content on spending some nicca's money instead of having her own. I guess she finally realized that all those designer clothes and fancy labels aren't the only thing life has to offer.

"I have a serious headache," Corset stated as she got out of my car. "I'm going to lay my ass down."

"I thought you were going to meet with the wedding planner with me."

"That shit has to wait. I'll meet her next time. Fill me in on what she said when I wake up. The way my attitude is set up right now, I'm sure you wouldn't want me assisting you with shit."

"You have a point. Go lay down and feel better."

Corset took my key out my hand and went inside. I was about to walk behind her when someone called my name. I looked around and saw Detective Fischer walking towards me. I hadn't seen her since the arson.

"Hey, Barbie. Do you have a minute?"

"Sure. Do you want to come inside?"

"No, it won't take too long. I just want you to be aware that a few of your neighbors are concerned. A woman dressed in all black has been spotted lurking around. Strange cars have been spotted too. Have you heard or seen anything out of the ordinary?"

"No. I was at my parent's house for a little while, so I probably missed all the action."

"How about Benz? How is he doing now that his home is back in order?"

"He's adjusting. We both are. We were in a car accident last week, so things have been a little traumatic recently."

"I'm sorry to hear that," Detective Fischer said genuinely. "I hope you both are doing alright."

"We are. Thanks for your concern."

"Well, I won't take up any more of your time. I just wanted you to be aware of what's going on in the neighborhood, and I wanted to get an update on how things were going after the fire."

"Say have you all caught the woman who did this to Benz's place?"

"No, we haven't. However, the woman that the neighbor's described lurking around sounds like the same woman who committed arson."

"Wow. That's scary."

"It is. We intend to catch her this time before she can cause any more trouble."

"I sure hope so."

The detective nodded. "Have a nice day."

I watched her as she walked away. I turned around, and I was nearly scared to death when I bumped right into Che.

"Goodness," I said, grabbing my chest. "Why didn't you say something? I didn't even know you were standing there."

The shit was creepy. Was she watching me talk to the detective?

"My apologies. I was about to tap you on the shoulder when you spun around."

"Call out my name next time so I won't be startled."

"Duly noted. Was that the police?"

"Yes," I answered.

"Are you okay?"

"Oh, I'm fine. Let's go inside."

"Yes. I agree. I have limited time, and I want to make up for leaving so suddenly last time."

Che followed me inside and I made sure to lock my door since I knew the crazy woman was back in the neighborhood. We sat down in my office, chatting about her ideas for the wedding. As she expressed what she thought I might like, I skimmed through her wedding book that she bought.

"This is some really nice work," I admired. "You definitely have a gift."

"Thank you. I have three appointments booked for you. Since you already have the venue, I want you to visit the flower shop and speak with the florist. Next you have a fitting for your wedding dress with the bridesmaids. Third, the cake tasting. In between those appointments, I will be sending you pictures of decorations. Oh, and one last thing, have you picked your wedding colors yet."

"Yes. Benz and I will be wearing all white. I was thinking more of a traditional look. The wedding party will be in black and white. And the decorations will be white, black, silver and gold."

"Nice. I like that. Those are classic colors and easy to find. I'm going to have a blast organizing your wedding."

"I hope so. I'm still sort of nervous."

"Don't be. I got you covered."

I smiled and sighed in relief. As quirky as she was, she knew her shit. I was grateful I didn't have to plan this shit. I wouldn't have any help at all. Corset is all I have and that heffa is upstairs sleep. I would be getting married in pajamas if it was left up to her.

"If you don't have any more questions, that'll be all for now."

I walked Che to the door. "Thanks again. I couldn't do this without you."

"No problem. I'm glad to be of service."

She winked at me and left.

# Chapter 18

## Barbie Bennett

"So, how did things go between you and Cake?"

Corset rolled her eyes at me so hard it looked like they fell out of her head. "Ask Tishika."

"Who is that?"

"The ghetto ass bitch that he fucks around with when he's not with me."

"Damn. I thought Benz and I had problems."

"Girl, Cake and I are over. I'm going to focus on my shit and leave that nicca alone. All he likes is birds and I'm not nobody's bird."

"I'm sorry, Set. I was rooting for y'all."

"Yeah. Me too. I mean, we're still cool. I'm just not interested in having a relationship with him."

"What if he gets his shit together? Then would you consider?"

Corset turned up her lips. "I might. Don't get me wrong,

Barbie. I have mad love for him, and I always will, but he's not going to keep treating me like I don't matter. I deserve more and if he can't give it to me, then the next nicca will."

"Cut his ass some slack, Set. He's been through a lot. He's still recovering from being kidnapped. Give him some time. He'll come around."

"I said we're still friends. That's all I can do for the nicca. I ain't cut his ass off because I know he's going through some shit. We still talk and whatnot. I'm just not trying to be his side piece anymore."

"I hear you, but you've said that before. The minute you need some dick, you were right back in Cake's bed. The attraction between you too is insane."

"That's true. He got a mean stroke game." Corset grinned as if she was thinking about her last time with Cake. "I can admit his pipe is on point. He hits all the right spots and then some."

"Like I said, you'll be back in his bed."

"Damn, Barbie, I'm trying to be strong. Can't you have my back like I have yours?"

"Okay, my bad, cuzo. I do have your back. No matter what you decide, I got you. If you go back to Cake or leave him for good, I'm going to be here with you no matter what."

"Thank you. Let's not forget how many times I've listened to your endless rants about Benz and how much you loved him, but didn't want to tell him, and he was with some bitch."

It was my turn to sigh. She had a point. "You're right."

"I know. Now, where is this wedding planner? This bitch needs to come on. I got shit to do."

It seemed like the moment Corset said that Che whipped into the parking lot of the bakery.

"There she goes right there," I pointed.

"It's about time. She acts like we're on her time instead of her being on ours. I would ask for a discount."

I giggled. "Can you please be on your best behavior? She is planning my wedding."

Corset cut her eyes again. "I guess. These cakes better be good or I'ma have an attitude. I left school in a rush to meet up with you, so I'm hungry."

"I'll buy you dinner after this. How does that sound?"

"Anything, I want?" Corset asked with a smirk.

"Damn, Set, your ass is pushing it."

She winked at me. "I know exactly what I want."

"It bet not be expensive. You know a bitch is still on medical leave, which means, I don't have money to blow like that."

"I know, but Benz does. You'll be alright," she chided, walking into the bakery before me. "As much as that nicca put you through, you better break his pockets on this wedding. Buy the most expensive tier cake they got."

I laughed because I knew Corset was dead ass serious. She loved Benz like a brother, but she was always going to be my rider. Cousins for life.

Sweet Extreme Bakery definitely lived up to its name. This place was fabulous. I had never heard of them before, but I wasn't into buying fancy cakes or tiered cakes before now. For birthday parties or special occasions either my mother or my aunt made the cake or we went to Jewels. However, I was glad Che introduced me to this gorgeous place. It looked like it was fit for a queen.

"Hello. Welcome to Sweet Extreme. Do you have a reservation?"

Corset looked at me. "Fancy, huh?"

I nudged her with my elbow.

Che spoke up for us. "Yes. Cake tasting for Barbie."

"Oh yes," the hostess stated. "Right this way. I have a room waiting for you. "I do apologize. We have a lot of weddings this time of year. Normally, you would have a room to yourself, but we had to book two tastings to a room tonight."

"As long as I get to taste my cakes, that shouldn't be a problem," I voiced.

Che and the hostess chatted for a moment before she waved at me and Corset and left. The hostess turned to me and spoke again.

"Thank you for being so understanding. Should you decide

to pick our bakery, we will gladly give you fifteen percent off the regular price due to the inconvenience."

Corset grinned. "I like this place already. You know how I feel about customer service."

"We wouldn't have it any other way," the snooty hostess said as she led us to our tasting room.

As we walked further into the bakery, we saw families enjoying pastries together. Everyone had a smile on their face as they licked icing from their fingers or wiped the sugary goodness from their mouths.

"Did you see how those people were licking their fingers?" Corset asked when we sat down.

"Yes, crazy ass, I did. Don't embarrass me."

"Shit, I'ma try not to, but I told your ass I'm hungry. I need a large cake tasting."

I giggled. "Ain't no such thing and you know it. We get small portions. That's why it's called a tasting."

Corset looked at me crazy. "Whatever. They better make a damn exception before I act a fool."

"You better not," I reprimanded. "We are not here for your greedy ass. This is for my wedding."

Corset tsked. "Okay. I heard you. Wedding vibes only."

"You damn right," I scolded.

The host returned with a beautiful display with two trays for us. It had six cupcakes a piece for us to taste.

"Thank you."

"You're quite welcome. Before I go to get the guests that will be joining you in this room, would you like milk or water to go with the tasting?"

"Can we have both?" Corset asked."

"Yes, of course. Someone else will be bringing it to you, but I assure you I will be back once I get the other guests seated and bring out their tasting."

"No problem," I said, bucking my eyes at Corset who was already on her second cupcake.

When the hostess left, I spoke again. "Can't take your ass nowhere."

"Girl, I'm not thinking about you. I said I was hungry."

"I hope you're thinking about the flavors while you're chowing down on those cupcakes."

"I am. So far, I like the pineapple and the mango coconut."

I stared at my cupcakes. I hadn't taken one bite. I decided on the vanilla and the chocolate just to see what they had to offer. "Hmmm. The regular flavors are good too."

"They are. This is going to be a hard decision. All of them taste good. I'm glad I'm not you right now because I would have an assorted rainbow flavored cake with all these flavors."

"You got a point. This is a hard decision. Maybe I can pick three flavors since it's a three-tier cake."

"Make it a four-tier cake and you can have four out of six."

I stared at Corset and she shrugged.

"I'm just saying. Make your job easier and please your guests at the same time.

"You got a point. I might just do that. Two plain like vanilla and chocolate and two tropical flavors."

"Now, you're talking."

The hostess returned with two ghetto looking chicks sitting them in the room with us. Corset was smashing her last cupcake, so she didn't notice them, but I did. They looked ratchet as fuck, and I didn't want to be in the room with them. They both had resting bitch faces, and I could tell that they were going to be a problem. The way Corset's attitude was set up, it would only be a matter of time before these two ghetto ass bitches got on her nerves. Right now, she was happy enjoying her cupcakes.

The hostess came back with our milk and water. "Which one is your favorite?" she asked

"I like the pineapple," I boasted.

"I like them all," Corset commented, licking her fingers, one by one.

"Very well. That means we have done our job here if you can't decide. I'll give you ladies a little more time."

The hostess left and that's when all hell broke loose.

"I know that ain't that bitch over there?" one of the ghetto looking chicks from across the room said.

They were both pretty, but I could see the ratchetness a

mile away.

Before I could even diffuse the situation, Corset was already looking at me. "I know them hoes wasn't talking about one of us."

"Just ignore them," I said. "I'm trying to keep the peace." I knew Corset wasn't going to let the shit go, but I tried.

"Peace?" Corset looked at me like I just spit on her. "I wish I would." She spun around in her chair so fast, I thought she was going to hit the floor. "Awe, hell naw. I know this bitch ain't up in here."

"Takes a bitch to know a bitch," the most ratchet one said. She was a light skin chick with freckles and red hair. Kind of cute, but strange looking. Not to mention her attitude sucked ass.

"Who is that? You know that chick?" I asked, confused as hell.

"Yes, I know that bitch," Corset said, jumping to her feet, knocking over her chair. "That's that bitch Tishika I was telling you about."

I gasped because I knew there was no way I was going to be able to stop Corset from fucking Tishika up.

"Cake is mine," Tishika hollered angrily.

"Bitch, he wants me not you," Corset yelled. "That's why every time he kisses you, it's my pussy juice that you taste."

"Oh yeah," Tishika said, throwing a cupcake at Corset.

What did she do that for? Corset kicked off her heels and

took off her earrings, ready to fuck her up.

"Bring it on, bitch. I've been waiting to beat your ass."

"Make it do what it do, bitch."

Tishika's friend stood back just like I did and let them go at it. I already knew what time it was, but I'm not sure Tishika did. Corset loves her some Cake. She would go to the ends of the earth for him. No matter how much she complained about him, I knew he was her soft spot, which meant she would fuck a bitch up over the man. Moon was her past love, but Cake was her present love. Tishika didn't stand a chance.

They both got into a fighting stance, circling each other with their fists balled up. Tishika swung first and missed. Corset caught her slipping and hit her with a one-two punch. Tishika looked dazed for a minute, but recovered quickly, punching back. One of her two punches connected with Corset, but what she didn't see coming was the kick that Corset had waiting for her.

When Corset's foot connected with Tishika's side, she was done for. Tishika went down like a dead body. Corset took full advantage of her vulnerability, jumping on top of her, punching her in the face. Tishika kept pulling at Corset's long hair, but it wasn't a match for the punches that she received to the face.

Her friend thought she was going to jump in and I had to stop the bitch. "We fight fair around here. If you want to tag in, then I will too, and you'll get your ass beat too. It's up to you."

# Princess Diamond

I rolled up my sleeves and took my earrings out just in case her friend was about to get buck. Her friend looked at me and then back at Corset and Tishika. I gave her a look that said *don't try me bitch*. She gulped hard and stayed still. I was hoping that she would jump because I was ready to fuck her up.

The hostess came back into the room and nearly had a heart attack. Corset and Tishika were still going at it. Although, I was proud because my cousin was beating the brakes off Tishika. I know her friend wanted to jump in. Every time she thought about it, I cracked my knuckles and gave her a sinister look. She wasn't crazy so she fell back. The hostess blew a whistle and everyone froze.

"I can't believe what's going on in here," she exclaimed. "I ought to terminate your contracts."

That's when I had to speak up. "Wait a minute. We were doing fine until these two ghetto bunnies showed up."

The hostess looked at Tishika and her friend. "You know what, she has a point. I got a bad vibe from the moment you two came in here. I knew it was going to be some problems. You two have to leave."

Corset got off of Tishika and came to stand by me while Tishika's friend rushed to her aid.

"They came at us," Tishika lied.

The hostess pointed her finger at them two. "Take it up with the manager."

The hostess called out for some burly ass nicca who came with back up. It was three of them, and they picked up Tishika and her friend, carrying them out.

"I'ma see you again, bitch," Tishika said to Corset, kicking and screaming.

"I'll be ready once again to beat your ass, bitch."

I shook my head as Corset gathered her things.

"Before you say anything," Corset said. "I didn't start the shit. Them bitches did."

"I agree. Let's go home. I'm tired."

"Not yet heffa. You owe me dinner."

"True. Will Uber eats be cool?"

"As long as I get to order what I want."

"Deal."

# Chapter 19

## Brysen "Benz" Sorensen

I was chilling in the trap with my crew. I stopped by to see how these niccas were really doing. Every time I asked them how things were going, I got one-word answers. That shit didn't sit well with me. In the back of my mind, I heard the opposite of what they were telling me. My intuition told me to stop by. No matter how high up the food chain I got, I was never above stopping at the trap to check on my investment.

As soon as I got out of my car, I was recognized. The block greeted me. I said my what ups and made my way inside. After checking the place out, things seemed to be on point. The product was being bagged and ready for shipment. The corner boys were on the lookout and making moves accordingly.

"Yo!" I announced myself, walking into the room.

My lieutenant and his crew stood up and gave me the respect that I deserved. After we dapped it up and handed out hugs, everyone took a seat on the couch or the chairs surrounding the PlayStation.

"What you doing here, boss man?"

"Checking on my money. Shit, you know I don't trust you niccas."

They laughed and I laughed too. I might have found humor in what was said, but I was damn serious about my money. I was chatting it up with them when Traffik appeared in the doorway. He didn't say anything, but from the look on his face, I could tell that shit wasn't right.

"I'll be back," I told my lieutenant and his crew, walking out of the room, out of the trap to Traffik's car. As soon as I got in, he spoke.

"Take a ride with me."

I nodded and we both put on our seatbelts. Twelve stayed out here trying to catch a nicca slipping. Traffik drove until he reached a secluded alley way with two abandoned houses surrounding it.

"The fuck is out this way?"

"You'll see."

He got out of the car and I did too. I took out my gun as we walked around to the trunk of the car. At this point, I didn't know what to expect so anybody could get it, including his muthafuckin' ass. Traffik was my boy, but I had no idea what this nicca was on right now.

Traffik popped the trunk. I stared inside wondering who

this nicca was. "Who this?"

"The nicca that was around the way talking shit about Cake."

"Oh word?" He had my full attention now.

"Yeah. I had been watching this nicca for a minute now. He thought he was the shit, popping off and whatnot."

"Is that right?" I asked. "What the nicca say?"

"A lot. He said he knew who was really after Cake and that we didn't kill the real snitch. That's why we need to go to the warehouse."

I nodded and Traffik closed the trunk. I knew why he did what he did. He wanted to show me that we weren't on some bogus mission. I'm glad he did because on the low, I was starting to get suspicious of his ass. Fucking around with the streets, anybody could get it.

Traffik went to the warehouse that I owned, in a fake name of course. We got out again. This time when he popped the trunk, he grabbed the dude out and drug his ass inside of the warehouse, slamming him down in a chair. He snatched the duct tape off of his mouth and the man screamed.

"Tell me what the fuck I need to know?"

The nicca winced and I wanted to pop his ass.

Traffik fell back and let me do my thing.

"Wh...wha...what do you want to know?"

"Tell me what you said about my cousin?"

"Who is your cousin?"

"I don't have time for games," I announced, letting off a shot."

It hit dude in the shoulder. Traffik looked at me and I shrugged.

"My bad. I thought it was going to be his arm.

"A little bit to the right and you would have popped his ass in the neck. Then we wouldn't have any information."

"You have a point. I'll be more careful."

I had to slow down with my trigger-happy ass.

"The fuck you know about my cousin's kidnapping?" I asked.

"Who is your cousin?"

"Nicca don't try to play me. I'm not in the mood. I will kill your ass."

Dude glared at me as if he had no clue.

"Cake, nicca. I heard you had his name in your mouth."

"Man, fuck your cousin, nicca."

I was about to chill out when he pushed my button.

"Chill," I heard Traffik say, but it was too late.

Before I knew it, I had raised my gun and shot that nicca twice in both eyes.

"Muthafucka. I hope you watch who you fuckin' talk to like that in hell. Clean this nicca up," I demanded.

"We didn't get any information," Traffik urged.

"Fuck it. I'll find another way. This nicca was too damn disrespectful, and I'm not in the mood."

My phone had been going crazy while I was interrogating that pussy ass nicca. I looked at my call log and noticed that I had four missed calls from Barbie and a text message.

**Barbie: I hope you didn't forget that you were supposed to meet the wedding planner today. You better not be on no bullshit. Call me back.**

I called her back, but I got her voicemail, so I texted her instead,

**Me: Sorry, babe. I just tied up some loose ends and I'm on my way home now.**

**Barbie: Hurry up. You should be here by now.**

I hopped into my ride and tossed my phone on the seat. I had no interest in this wedding shit. I have told Barbie a million times that I just wanted to show up with the ring and say my vows. All this extra shit was her thing, not mine. No matter how much I expressed my lack of interest, she still wanted to include me so here I was.

I used my spare key to open the front door, hearing voices in Barbie's living room. I was about to walk in and join her, announcing that I was here, but something stopped me. The other voice. I stepped back before either one of them could see me. No. That can't be who the fuck I think it is.

Taking another peek, I saw Dache clearly. This bitch was

sitting in Barbie's living room talking to her like a long-lost friend. I want to spazz the fuck out because I thought this bitch was dead. I guess she was the one who left the note on my car. My mind was blown because I never expected to see her again.

Quietly, I stepped backwards toward the door, slowly opening it, sneaking back out. I jumped back in my vehicle and parked further down the street so that I had a good look at Barbie's front door. I wanted a clear view to see when Dache's faking death ass walked out. As I waited for Dache to leave, I hit up Kapri.

"Yo, I just watched your last upload. You and Tec are dope. All them kill shots got me hype as fuck."

I chuckled. "Yo ass would like the kill shots."

He laughed.

"Listen, I need a favor."

"What's goodie?"

"Can you look up someone for me?"

"Yeah. Shoot me the information. I'll take care of it."

I texted him a little background information on Dache. Within minutes, he was hitting me back with her address and everything else I wanted to know about her ass. I circled the block and then parked down the street from where she lived. When I got out, a dude was already there sent by Kapri to hand me a key and the code to her spot. Being in cahoots with a Diaz-Santanas had its perks. I see why people joined their family's organization. They were very resourceful. It was a win-win situation.

The dude gave me that look. I knew time was of the essence. I had to get in and get out. Do what I had to do and bounce. That exactly what I intended to do. Walking into her apartment building, I made sure my face was covered with a mask and transition glasses. Smoothly, I let myself into the building and hid my face from the camera as I waited for the elevator. With gloves and precision, I let myself into Dache's new apartment.

I didn't see any signs of her kids here. Unlike the last place where she had baby stuff in view. I don't know what she did with her kids and I didn't care. I just hoped that maybe they were with their father or fathers or maybe their grandmother because tonight she was going to die.

With my gloves already on, I took my hammer out of my jacket pocket and went to work destroying her place from room to room. I thought about how she played me, and the rage continued to boil over until she came home Boldly, I was sitting on her couch waiting for her ass to walk in. Gun pointed in her direction and all. She didn't even see me until she closed the door and locked it. That's when I cocked the gun.

"What are you doing here?" she had the nerve to ask me.

"What the fuck are you planning a wedding with my fiancée for?

"Nicca, you have a lot of nerve asking me anything. The last time I saw you, I was being shot at."

"Speaking of that, the last time I saw your triflin' ass you were being thrown into the ocean. Imagine my surprise to see you still alive."

"Surprise," she said, walking further into the apartment. This bitch was bold as fuck. She could have run out the door, but I'm sure she realized that she would have been shot dead on the spot so she made the right choice.

"Have a seat," I patted the space next to me.

Dache sauntered across the room, flopping down next to me.

"I got questions.

Dache sighed. "What is that?"

"You already know. I'm not here to play games. Tell me what I need to know. Why are you still alive?"

Dache sighed. I knew what she was going to say would be a doozy. "The bullet you shot me with hit my planner."

"Bullshit," I called out.

"No. Hear me out."

"Okay. You have my attention."

"The truth is I was contracted to take you out."

"By who?"

"That's the part I'm not sure about. I was told to say Archie, but I'm not sure if it was really him."

"Why do you say that?"

"Things just don't add up. The woman who asked me to kill you said that Archie hired me."

"The woman?" I asked. "What did she look like?"

"I'm not sure. She was masked up with fake everything. After our initial meeting, I never saw her again. She wired me the money."

"Let's run this shit from the beginning. I need to know everything."

The shit Dache told me blew my muthafucking mind. She told me that she was the one who broke into my crib, damaged my laptop, and set my place on fire to make shit look official. She knew about my warranty, and she knew that she would be assigned to my ticket and that I would get next to her. It was all a set up so that she could keep an eye on me while running game at the same time.

"What about the wedding planning shit? That sounds like a bit much. If you wanted to kill me, you would have just done it. Why go through so much trouble, hanging out with my fiancée?"

"Because after I failed to kill you the last time, the stakes were higher. The plan was for me to bomb your wedding."

"Say what now? What kind of terrorist bullshit are you on?"

"That's what the new contract was for. That's how I got this new apartment and money for my kids. Someone wants you dead real bad."

I was furious. This bitch wasn't shit, but I had something for her sneaky ass. While she was talking, I was texting Traffik. She might have lived last time, but she was going to die for sure this time. While her scary ass was rambling, Traffik and his crew showed up.

"Who are they?" Dache asked in fear.

"The niccas who are going to dispose of your body after I kill you."

I was going to make her death quick because she cooperated and told me what I wanted to know, but the bitch got froggy and leaped. With all these niccas in her spot, she jumped off the couch and attacked me. I fucked her ass up with that hammer. In midair, I hit that bitch right in the face. The force of the hammer caught her in the eye, stopping whatever the fuck she thought she was about to do.

"Bitch!" I yelled as Traffik and his boys laughed. "I was going to make this quick, but you done fucked up now."

I completely snapped. I hit her with that hammer until I got tired. I didn't give a fuck if I had blood on me or not. She got the ass beating of a lifetime. When I got done pounding her face in with the hammer, she was nothing but blood and brains. Literally, Traffik, had to pull me away from her mangled body.

I'm glad I called him because he came prepared, handing me wipes to clean off the blood, and a jumpsuit and shoes. He knew me well. He knew I was going to lose control. That's why he was on my team.

"Make sure her kids are taken care of," I commanded before I left.

# Chapter 20

# Barbie Bennett

This nicca said he was on his way a while ago. I had been calling and texting and texting and calling Benz's black ass. He had been moving real funny lately. That's what made me think he was cheating. Don't know niccas that stay in the streets like that unless its pussy involved. I tried to give him the benefit of the doubt, but I felt like he was back to his old ways.

"Which one did you like?" Che asked me.

"Uh?"

I had my face glued to my phone, trying to figure out where Benz was. He said he would be here. The fact that he wasn't getting back to me had me worried. The thought that something might have happened to him did cross my mind, but my gut told me that he was avoiding me.

"They both look nice," I mumbled while texting people to see if they had heard from Benz.

I was pissed when I heard he was at the trap. All them hoes

they be having up in that muthafucka. Bitches just waiting in line to suck dick. My blood pressure went up every time he took his ass over that way. I'm sure it was a slew of hoes ready to replace me. With Benz's hoe record, he probably fucked around with all of them back in the day.

"You seem distracted," Che stated.

"I'm sorry I am. My mind is all over the place. My fiancé said he was on his way and it's been over an hour since I heard from him."

"We can reschedule if you like."

She must've read my mind because I was just about to throw her ass out.

"That would be best," I exclaimed.

Che packed up her things. "Everything has been arranged except for the flower arrangements. If you liked them both, I can just pick one so you can handle whatever personal issue you need to attend to."

"Sounds like a plan."

I remained calm until Che left, and then I screamed at the top of my lungs. Benz done fucked up. I was prepared when his ass finally came home. I mean, I popped off my nails, put my weave up in a bun, Vaseline on my face, and sat down with a damn knife like a psycho in the living room while sipping on a glass of wine.

"Where the fuck you been?" I screamed as soon as Benz

walked in, waving the big knife at him as I spoke.

"Why the hell are you waving a knife at me?"

"Because I'm going to Lorena Bobbitt your dick nicca," I spat, waving the knife at him again.

He jumped back, and I would have laughed if I wasn't so angry.

"What's wrong with you woman?"

"Where were you?"

"Handling business."

"Sure," I scoffed. "And I was sitting here about to cook with this knife instead of stabbing your ass."

"Yo, you need to chill the fuck out and put the knife down. I got something to tell you."

I shifted my stance ready to slice his ass up as soon as he admitted to cheating.

Benz was about to speak and then he stopped. "I know you don't think I was out cheating?" he asked, staring at the big, sharp knife I was holding. It was as if he had just read my mind.

"I sure do. And I'm waiting for you to say it so I can stab the shit out of your ass."

Benz glared at me and I couldn't read his expression. 'Look at me," he said, turning around. "Have you even noticed that I'm not wearing the same shit I had on when I left? Huh? You're so fuckin' quick to accuse me of doing some foul shit when you can't see what's right in front of your eyes."

What he said made me pause. I blinked and then focused on what he was wearing. He looked like he just got out of jail. I dropped the knife on the floor and rushed over to him. "What happened?"

"I'm glad you finally came to your senses. I wasn't shit with that knife in your hand. Che is what happened. Your wedding planner."

"What? What did she do?"

"This bitch. I don't even know where to start with her ass."

My facial expression insisted on him explaining what he meant by his last statement.

"That bitch Dache is the one who broke into my shit, set it on fire, and fucked up my computer."

"You're lying," I said in disbelief.

"Hell no, I'm not. She's also the one who worked at the store where my computer had the warranty, so she worked on my ticket. Then, the bitch broke in that night that I rushed you off the phone."

"I remember that night because I was furious that you didn't call me back."

"Right. Well, now you know why. I shot the bitch and dumped her body."

"But she didn't die," I said completing his sentence. "So what made her become a wedding planner if she wanted to kill you?"

"You ain't gonna believe this shit. The bitch was going to bomb our wedding."

"Wow!" I said in shock.

"Exactly."

"Pack your shit," Benz demanded. "Fuck this wedding planning shit. We're going to Costa Rica. Far away from this shit here so we can get married in peace."

# Chapter 21

## Barbie Bennett

Corset and I walked into the room and saw Cake and Benz waiting for us. I ran over to Benz, hugging and kissing him. He came earlier to make sure everything was all set up for our big day.

"Baybeeee, this room is so nice," I beamed.

Benz winked. "You mean suite, my love. Rooms are for losers."

"They got a damn spa," Corset said. "I can't wait to get a massage. It's included in the package."

"It is?" Cake asked, snatching the brochure from Corset.

"You didn't have to snatch, bone head ass nicca." Corset popped cake in the head with the other brochure that was next to the phone.

"We out," Cake said, grabbing, Corset by the hand. "Let's get a massage and visit our room,"

"Our?" Corset wondered. "I'm not staying with your ass."

"Yes, ours. I know you didn't think we were going to be in separate rooms."

"Yes, I did. We're not together, remember?"

Cake moved in close and whispered something into Corset's ear. Whatever he said made her change her mood immediately. She was giggling and blushing while he caressed her back and nibbled on her ear. Next thing I knew, they were out of our suite.

I sat down on Benz's lap. I wish all of our family members could have been here like we planned."

Benz rubbed my hand gently. "Everyone that's supposed to be here is here."

"You're right. Are you nervous?"

"A little, but I know I'm doing the right thing. I've loved you for a long time."

"Oh really. Before or after I confessed my love to you?"

"Before. I was just in denial. I'm glad you made the first move, or we might still be friends."

"Awww, baby."

I leaned in for a kiss and before I knew it, Benz and I were all over each other. It was getting too hot and heavy. I had to scoot away.

"We'll be married in a few hours. In fact, you're not even supposed to be in here."

"You're right. Let me go check on the rest of the family.

Besides, I got a surprise for you."

"What is it?" I shrieked.

"You'll see."

"I'm going to go and get it right now."

Benz got up and left and I fell back on the couch, feeling like the happiest woman. The suite was so large that there was a his and her quarters. We could get dressed in the same room without seeing each other. As I was relaxing, the door opened up and the least likely person I expected to see walked in.

"Hey," Rozi mumbled.

I sat up, staring at her, not knowing what to expect.

"You're probably surprised to see me."

I nodded, not wanting to say anything to offend her.

"I wouldn't miss your wedding day. I know how much you love Benz."

"I do."

Rozi rushed over to me and I braced myself. She moved so fast I thought she was going to attack me. Instead, she hugged me tight and kissed me on the cheek.

"I'm sorry, cuzo. I was tripping. I was all in my feelings as if you had shot Sab personally."

"I know you were hurt. I just feel so bad that something so awful happened to him."

"Oh, cuzo."

"Oh, cuzo."

We rocked back and forth, hugging each other lovingly. Rozi and I chopped it up, apologizing to each other a million more times, and cried a dozen more. She had to reapply my make up twice due to all of the crying that I had done. After a couple of hours, I was ready to take things to the next level with my future husband.

Malice's nieces were the cutest little flower girls, throwing roses in the sand before the bridesmaids and groomsmen followed. Sabre and Rozi walked down the sandy beach first. Then, Cake and Corset. Finally, Malice used his cane to slowly walk towards Benz with Behati helping him take his place as best man. The wedding music started, and my father locked his arm with mine and began walking me down the sand to the man that I loved.

My father helped me up the steps of the make-shift altar handing me over to Benz. They nodded at each other, and I held back tears trying not to cry. I took my place across from Benz and smiled at Malice's kids, both of our fathers, my mother, and our grandparents. They were the only other guests invited. Benz didn't want to take the chance of anyone else ruining the wedding, so only a limited amount of people were invited.

The preacher began. "Dearly beloved. We are gathered here today in celebration of this holy union of Barbie and Brysen. Two wonderful people who have prepared their own vows."

The preacher looked at me and a lump formed in my throat.

I was so anxious. I swallowed the lump and proceeded to say my vows.

"I, Barbie, take you Brysen to be my husband. To love, honor, and respect. God created me to be with you and only you. I will be yours forever and ever."

The preacher turned towards Benz, nodding at him that it was his turn.

"I, Brysen, take you Barbie to be my wife. To love, honor, and respect you forever. I belong to you and I'm proud to say that you belong to me. I promise to protect and love you like no other man will. My love for you is infinite."

The preacher spoke again. "You may now exchange the rings."

Corset handed me Benz's ring which I placed on his finger. Malice handed Benz his ring which he placed on my finger.

"With these vows, the exchanges of the rings, and in the eyes of God, I now pronounce you husband and wife. Mr. and Mrs. Sorensen."

I saw a tear fall from Benz's eye. I wiped it away and kissed my husband. That felt so good to say the word husband. Lord knows I went through hell and high water to get this man to be mine. In the end, I guess I can say it was all worth it. I finally have his last name.

"Who is ready to party?" Cake said, clapping.

"Meeee," Corset said, joining in. "Malice and Behati

planned a beautiful ceremony. However, Cake and I planned the reception and it's going to be lit. I'm ready to get drunk and be merry."

*•.¸♡ **Barbie & Benz** ♡¸.•*

Benz staggered as he carried me through the door of our suite. He was tipsy as fuck while I was sober as could be.

"I feel like you've gained weight. How much have you eaten on medical leave? You might want to go on a diet."

I practically jumped out of his arms, slapping him in the chest. "Benz, that's not nice. I have a reason why I've gained weight."

I reached into my clutch and handed him a bracelet box.

"How nice. You got me a gift."

"Open it," I grinned.

Benz's eyes glowed with anticipation as he opened the box revealing the positive pregnancy test. It took him a moment to realize it wasn't jewelry. After he picked the stick up and stared at it, he gasped.

"You're pregnant?" he quizzed with surprise.

"Yes!" I confirmed.

"Hell yeah! I knew it," he gloated with a fist pump in the air. "I hit just right the last time."

"You didn't know shit. Just a moment ago, you were telling

me I was fat, and I needed to diet."

"No. I was just kidding."

I smacked my lips. "You're such a liar."

Benz looked at me, cracking up laughing. "I'm too damn fucked up to lie."

I stepped closer to him, shedding my reception dress. "Are you going to stand there laughing, or are you going to come and get some of this sweet pregnant pussy."

Benz straightened up real quick. "Sweet pussy it is."

Benz nearly ripped his suit trying to get it off.

We embraced each other, kissing passionately. Our tongues danced inside of our mouths while our hands did the same to our bodies. I grabbed my husband's bulge, rubbing his dick gently. I wanted to tell him to take it slow so I could savor every moment. Then again, I was ready to get it on. I was horny as hell. I couldn't wait to have Benz's dick inside of me, but I needed to taste him first.

I opened my mouth, swirling my tongue around the tip of his dick. Holding his thick member with both of my hands, I stroked him while licking the shaft with my wet mouth. Continuing to jerk him off, I devoured his tool and tickled the back of my throat with the tip.

Benz let out a groan and pushed me away. I smirked because I was sure he couldn't take it anymore. I laid down on the bed, opening my waxed pussy, playing in it as Benz stared at me lustfully. I knew he was trying to regain his composure, but this was our honeymoon, so I planned on tempting him every step of the way.

He positioned himself between my legs and slowly pushed the tip inside. My body jerked. I was craving for his manhood.

"Oh, Benz, fuck me."

Suddenly, he pulled out and began, licking my sweet spot between my legs. He kissed all around my clit and then devoured it like a seafood dinner. Before my body could convulse again, he stopped sucking, thrusting his dick back inside of me. Roughly, he rammed into me. I bucked my hips at him, moaning louder. My moans became cries of passion as I orgasmed. Benz grunted loudly and fell on top of me. His body stiffened as he climaxed too.

"That shit was good as fuck," Benz groaned.

I giggled. "Married sex is the best sex."

"Sure is. Give me like ten minutes, and I'll be ready for round two."

"Yes, husband."

Benz turned his head to face me. "I bet you couldn't wait to call me your husband."

"You damn right. I earned this title as your wife."

# Chapter 22

## Brysen "Benz" Sorensen

Everyone was wore the hell out on the trip coming back from Costa Rica. I'm not sure what everyone else did during the entire trip that made them tired, but I can tell you what Barbie and I did. We fucked all over the place. She made me wait so I needed to get as much pussy as possible, making up for lost time.

We went night walking and fucked. We went hiking and fucked. We swam in the waterfall and got our freak on in that bitch too. Besides fucking most of the time, Barbie and I managed to explore the beautiful land with our families too. We also spent quite a bit of time at the beach. The honeymoon was everything, but now we were on our way back home.

"Did you enjoy your time, Mrs. Sorensen?" I asked Barbie. She loved when I addressed her by her new last name.

We were sitting in our private lounge on the jet, relaxing. She snuggled closer to me with her head on my shoulder.

Looking down at my hand, I stretched my fingers, enjoying the sparkle of my diamond wedding ring. "I sure did."

"Me too. I wish we could have stayed longer, but I need to get back. Business as usual."

"I know right. My leave is practically up. I need to make arrangements to go back into the office."

"How do you feel about that? Are you ready?"

"As ready as I'm going to be."

"What about our living arrangements?"

"I hadn't thought about that. I was so excited to get married that I didn't realize all the things we'd have to get rid of and combine."

"I think we should move into one condo and sell the other one."

"Or we could keep it and rent it out."

"True, but which one though? I've lived at both so it will be hard for me to decide."

Barbie kissed my cheek. "It doesn't matter to me. We can move into either one. As long as we're together."

"Awww, babe. That was so sweet."

"Are you mocking me?" Barbie asked, slapping my chest.

"No. I really thought that was sweet. Give me a kiss."

Barbie lifted her head and pecked my lips.

"I want another one."

# Princess Diamond

This time when she kissed me, I gave her a little tongue. Kissing, touching, and rubbing lead to a mile-high quickie. We had to sneak and get it in. Our parents were on this plane. I would be mortified if they heard us.

Once we got our freak on, we ate our food, and watched a chick flick. I would never agree to this shit on the regular, but Barbie was wifey now. I had to compromise. Besides, this was going to be my leverage in the long run. I compromised now, she would have to compromise later.

### *•.,♡ Barbie & Benz ♡,.•*

Barbie nudged me. "Baby, we're home."

I stretched and stood up. Most of our family was already walking towards the door. We were the last ones to get off because our personal space was in the back. Barbie walked off the aircraft first and I followed, being the last one to exit. The car service was waiting for us. We rolled our luggage towards one of the many cars lined up to take us all home.

As soon as I was about to get into our car, all hell broke loose. Police cars surrounded the vehicle that Barbie and I were in. Officers jumped out with their guns drawn. The shit looked like something out of a movie. I was confused because I just knew they didn't have nothing on me.

Detective Rashan appeared before me. "Looks like you've finally fucked up, Benz. I got your ass. You're under arrest for the murder of Archie Abney."

To Be Continued....

Made in the USA
Las Vegas, NV
28 August 2021